THE SAM HOLI

Dying to Draw

Greed, murder, and revenge
in the Cotswolds

Honor Brightwell

Paperback ISBN: 978-1-0684791-0-6

eBook ISBN: 978-1-0684791-1-3

Published in the United Kingdom by Honor Brightwell.

Printed by Amazon.

Cover design by BespokeAuthor.com

For Beth Kempton.
Your wise words got me beyond the first page, and I am forever grateful.

Prologue

Saturday, January 22nd

The eerie, undulating sound of howling irritated his ears. Sleep-fogged, he assumed it was the wind. Now more awake, he realised there were no rattling windows or doors. No roar down the valley. The howl was pitched so that it stretched his nerves, making him want to shout 'stop'. And then he suddenly knew. It wasn't the wind. It was a dog. But who's dog? The only neighbour with a dog was Kaye, and her dog was generally quiet. A welcome 'woof' when you entered Kaye's cottage but not this constant—well, bawling. Almost of grief.

It wasn't yet light—January mornings were always slow starters—but sleep was impossible. Something was wrong. He reluctantly pushed the duvet aside, and reached for his jeans and fleece. He grabbed his phone, and went downstairs to find the large torch which he always kept on the windowsill near the front door. Strong winds often meant loss of power.

Stepping out of his cottage into the chill of the early morning, he instinctively pulled his fleece collar up closer around his neck. He glanced around him. No lights on in the other cottages. No street lights. No one else around. He turned on the torch and half ran out onto the lane towards Kaye's cottage. There were four properties, quite close together, all built with the grey stone that was so widely used for building in Cumbria in days gone by. Two were now holiday cottages, empty in January; one was Kaye's, and the other was his property.

Reaching Kaye's cottage, the last of the four, he lifted the door knocker. Robust as it was, its precise rat-a-tat-tat sounded too feeble, and he hammered on the door with his bare fists. Despite the noise, the door remained firmly closed and the howls changed to short, sharp barks.

'Gustav,' he called. 'It's me, Nate. What's up, boy? Why all the noise? Where's Kaye? Kaye? Can you hear me?' Kaye was silent, and all the dog could communicate was his misery. 'OK, I'm going round the back. See if I can get in.'

At least the howling had stopped, even though it was replaced by a gloomy whine. Tall bushes loomed up in the beam of his torch, casting shadows. He pushed the overhanging branches impatiently aside as he moved quickly to the back of the house.

'Kaye? Kaye? You in there?'

Nothing.

'I'm going to break a window and open the door,' he called in case anyone could hear him. He took off his fleece, shivering as the cold air hit the sweat on his body. Bending down, he found a large stone, wrapping the stone and his hand in the fleece. He hesitated, questioning if what he was about to do was really necessary. There was no other option. He struck the small pane near the door handle with a decisive blow. There was a crack and the sound of glass breaking. The key was in the lock on the inside of the door. Clumsy with his need to hurry while mindful of the jagged edges of glass, he fumbled to reach in and to turn the key. At last, the lock clicked back, and he breathed a sigh of relief. He was in.

The layout of Kaye's cottage was much the same as his. He knew the door ahead of him would open to the sitting room. Gustav rushed at him, with urgent, impatient barks. Patting Gustav and talking quietly to reassure him, he felt for the light switch. There was a sudden blast of brightness as the light came on. Nate's hand moved instinctively to cover his mouth as he part-gasped, part-choked on the rising bile. Before him, laid out on the hearth, was Kaye, her head haloed with blood. There was no doubt. Kaye was dead.

Chapter One

Monday, January 17th

The black line wiggled its way across the screen, half-heartedly nosing upwards and downwards a few times before straightening out to an abrupt stop. If it was a heartbeat, it would mean death. If it was a map, it would mean good news for anyone wanting a gentle walk or cycle ride. As a sales graph, it was a disaster.

Sam looked at the faces of the people around the meeting room table. It was her first day at Little Bear, the children's book publisher, and she wasn't yet sure what she'd got herself into. Melissa Bingley, author of the long-running *Granny Fi* series, looked outraged. Brendan McManners, Little Bear's Publishing Director, glared balefully at anyone unwise enough to meet his eye. A young editor (introduced as Amy Chang) and her colleague Jason Lee from the design studio, stared down at their notebooks in the hope this would make them invisible.

'Well, is anyone going to give me an explanation?' Melissa broke the silence, slapping the table top to emphasise 'anyone'. The gold bangles on her wrist rattled. Amy and Jason winced, and Brendan's already florid complexion darkened.

'At this point in the year,' Melissa continued, 'bookshops should be ordering in stock for the summer season, with the new *Granny Fi* story giving us a spike in sales for the whole series. That's what has always happened. But just look at that sales line: there hasn't been a single order!' With a final bang on the table, Melissa abruptly pushed back her chair and strode across to the coffee machine to refill her cup for the third time.

'Melissa, my dear,' began Brendan, but one look at Melissa made him immediately change tack. 'Look, it's tough times …'

'Rubbish. I've been following book sales for years, and I've never seen figures like these. The papers are full of articles about people buying more books during the pandemic—but not *Granny Fi* books, it seems! Why not?'

'Well, we're not in the pandemic now, are we, and people are spending money on other things. And I have been telling you for some time, Melissa, that *Granny Fi* has really had her day.'

'Had her day?' roared Melissa, earrings jangling, and cracks appearing in the vibrant lipstick at the corners of her mouth. '*Had her day?*' she hissed. '*Granny Fi* was the making of this publishing company, so if she's '*had her day*' then you, Brendan, have definitely had yours,' and she stabbed her index finger, tipped red with nail polish, at Brendan's perspiring face.

Brendan hurriedly sat further back in his chair as Melissa continued with 'perhaps we need a relaunch—new covers, new art, a new illustrator? Yes, Kaye's drawings are a bit outdated now,' and she looked expectantly at Jason, the designer, to agree with her, but he slid further down his chair.

Brendan sighed, and folded his hands over his expansive stomach. 'Melissa, we've talked about this before, and we haven't got a better illustrator on our books than Kaye. Her drawings *are* Granny Fi—we can't re-invent her after all these years.'

'Hmm, I'm not so sure.' Melissa replied. Her eyes suddenly alighted on Sam and narrowed slightly. 'You. You're marketing, aren't you? What's the marketing plan?'

'Er, well, um' stuttered Sam, looking to Brendan to explain just how new she was. But he simply smiled enquiringly at her and said

'Yes, what about the marketing plan? Do tell—er, Pam,' and folded his arms as though to ward off any entreaties for help.

'It's Sam, not Pam,' she explained but Brendan just waved his hand airily as though her name was of no importance.

'Well, it's my first day at Little Bear,' explained Sam, hoping this would buy her a little sympathy, 'and one of the reasons I wanted to join the company was because I wanted to work with the people who created Granny Fi ...'

'People?' queried Melissa, with not a trace of sympathy. 'It's not *people.* It's **me.** *I'm* the creator of Granny Fi. Without me there would not be any stories. Let me very clear about that. Brendan says Kaye made Granny Fi, but she couldn't create her without my stories. Got that? Right, carry on—and remember, you're not in the interview now. You've got the job, so what are you going to do about my sales?'

It was a good question, and one that Sam spent the afternoon thinking about. The sales of the *Granny Fi* series had flat-lined, and the future was not looking good for either the books, or for Little Bear. And perhaps not for Sam—unless she could come up with a plan.

As she worked her way through all the information she could find on *Granny Fi* she realised she'd reached the end of her first day. It had flown by, while at the same time it felt years since she got herself ready for work that morning. How excited she'd been—in fact, she'd had a bounce in her step ever since she got the call to say she'd got the job. She'd dressed for her first day in the clothes she had carefully chosen the night before (smart but not too smart, fashionable but not too trendy), and picked up her bag with everything she thought she'd need to get through her first day: new pen, new notebook, new water bottle. Nothing, however, had prepared her for the reality of her first meeting.

The Little Bear offices were within walking distance of her house in the small (but growing) Cotswold town of Lower

Rushford. It was a mild day (for January), and she stepped out briskly, smiling to herself at the prospect of the day ahead. Reaching the office building with its honey-coloured stone walls, she spun breezily through the revolving doors. The Little Bear logo, a small bear in silhouette, hung above the reception desk. A couple of well-worn chairs and a table with copies of some of Little Bear's books filled the space. Sam's nostrils twitched at the distinctive smells of books and furniture polish. She was going to love it here.

The receptionist looked up enquiringly, smiling at Sam's cheery 'Hello, I'm Sam Holliday, and this is my first day at Little Bear.' The receptionist made a brief call to the woman who would look after Sam on her first day, and soon Sam was whisked away. A quick tour of the offices introduced her to her new colleagues (hopefully nice), the facilities (basic), and the fire exit (scarily open ironwork stairs). All too soon she was left at her workstation, staring at a laptop screen.

'Hi, I'm Jen—Jen Somerville,' said a cheery voice.

'Hi, I'm Sam—Sam Holliday.'

'I thought you were. You're the new Marketing Manager, right? I work in marketing too. I was in a meeting when you had the guided tour.'

'Yes, that's me—the new Marketing Manager. I'm really excited about it. Can't wait to get started!' laughed Sam.

'Well, there's plenty for you to do—you're going to be busy. First up there's the meeting with Melissa and Brendan.'

'Oh yes, Brendan interviewed me. He seemed nice.'

'Really?' Jen replied, raising her eyebrows. Seeing Sam's puzzled frown, she added quickly 'um, well, I suppose he can be.'

'And Melissa?'

'Melissa Bingley. the …

'Creator of *Granny Fi*!' Sam finished for her. 'I can't wait to meet her! I'm such a fan of her stories.'

'She'll love you then! Be careful though—she's not always as sweet as Granny Fi!'

'What do you mean?' asked Sam.

Chapter One

'Tell me what you think of her after the meeting,' advised Jen with a knowing look.

'OK. So, where's the meeting, and when?' Sam asked as she ran her fingers through her thick, short hair, letting the curls fall naturally around the curve of her oval-shaped face.

'I'll show you,' offered Jen helpfully. 'Grab a coffee on the way?'

And now she'd not only survived her first meeting with Brendan and Melissa but she'd also got through her first day in her new job. Spinning the revolving door to go out into the January evening, Sam realised she wasn't feeling quite as excited as when she'd gone in that morning. Hands in her pockets, she trudged along the pavements thinking back over the day. Passing a row of houses with small front gardens, she noticed one had a large clump of snowdrops, the flowers peeking out shyly as though they expected someone might tell them to go away. Sam smiled—the first snowdrops of the year were always special, with their hint of new growth and the return of Spring. With a lighter step, she soon found herself back at her front door, which opened immediately into the sitting room of her small, two-bedroomed house.

Clicking on the lamp near the door, she looked appreciatively around the room as the soft light gave a warm glow to the simply furnished room. A comfy sofa and a couple of armchairs, a small table and shelves of books made it perfect as far as Sam was concerned. The mortgage had made her eyes water, but the small market town of Lower Rushford with its shops and railway line was, she thought, just where she wanted to live. With her new job the mortgage was affordable, and the cost was worth it to have her independence. Her 40th birthday had coincided with breaking off her long-standing relationship with Jack Henshaw. After five long years of living with him, she knew she needed her own space where she could regain her confidence to live in the way she wanted—free from ties, and without anyone telling her what she should be doing. Yes, Sam thought contentedly, this little house was just what she wanted—modern, easy to manage, and within walking distance of the office and the town's amenities.

Dropping her bag onto the nearest chair she walked through to the kitchen to put the kettle on. A cup of tea was just what she needed, and perhaps a biscuit or two to munch as she pondered her day, and what tomorrow might bring.

She'd just got settled on the sofa with her feet curled up under her when her mobile rang. From the ringtone she knew it was her mother, Elaine, no doubt calling to find out how her day had gone.

'Hi, Mum, how are you?' asked Sam.

'Never mind me, darling, what about you? How did your first day go? Do you love it as much as you thought you would?'

'Well …'

'Oh, no, what's happened?

'Well, it was quite challenging …' Sam faltered, thinking how she could describe the meeting to her mother.

'That's good though, isn't it? You get bored if you don't have a challenge.'

'True, but … well, there's a really nice woman in marketing called Jen. We seemed to click. But there are some very strong personalities, and I don't think the *Granny Fi* series is doing as well as I thought it was. You know how much I love those books, but it looks as though people are buying other things now,' said Sam.

'Oh. That wasn't what you expected, was it. Doesn't it just need some marketing—some posters in the bookshops or something, to get people buying again?' asked her mother.

Sam sighed. Sometimes she wished marketing was better understood. A few decorative posters were not going to reverse Little Bear's fortunes. But in a way, her mother did have a point.

'Maybe. I've got to come up with a plan. Melissa—Melissa Bingley, the *Granny Fi* author, wants to see it. She's a bit fierce—dressed to impress—not at all like Granny Fi,' said Sam, thinking that anyone less like dear Granny Fi would be hard to imagine.

'She'll soon see how brilliant you are.'

'Thanks for the vote of confidence, Mum! Granny Fi deserves a good plan, and if I can get the books selling then everyone's going to be happy—especially me!' added Sam with rather more confidence than she felt.

'That's my girl. All's fine here, by the way. Your father sends his love. I'll leave you to get on—I expect you've plenty to do.'

'I have, but thanks for calling, Mum. Speak soon!'

She really did have plenty to do. There was a meal to prepare, and a lot to think about. Her tea was cold and she decided she was now more in need of a glass of wine. She'd treated herself to a few bottles of white wine while holidaying in France last year, and this evening felt the right time to open one. There was a satisfying 'pop' as the cork came out—that sound always made her sigh with gentle pleasure. She poured a generous glass and savoured the aroma. Pears, honeysuckle … summer in a glass. Perfect for cheering up a dreary January.

Back on the sofa, she placed her glass carefully on the small table and rummaged in her bag for her notebook and pen. She needed to make a list of everything she'd learned today, and another list of everything she needed to do tomorrow—or at least by the end of the week. At the moment there were too many things whirling around in her head, and she knew that the lists would make her feel back in control.

Two glasses of wine later, she realised she hadn't yet eaten. She did, however, have two very long lists, and a slightly spinning head from drinking wine on an empty stomach. She padded out to the kitchen and looked in the fridge. An omelette maybe? She whisked eggs and chopped vegetables. There was some salad left from yesterday that would go with it. No bread, she noted. No butter either. '*Probably a good thing*,' she mused. She set a place at the breakfast bar and got her notebook to review her lists as she ate.

Looking over her notes from her first day, Sam realised she needed to understand the *Granny Fi* series better—not only as stories she loved, but as a money-generating brand for Little Bear. She had a lot of questions, and tomorrow, back in the office, she'd find the people who could give her some answers. In the meantime, Sam realised she desperately needed some sleep.

Chapter Two

Tuesday, January 18th

Early birdsong broke through Sam's sleep, and she snuggled deeper into the duvet, not yet ready to be an early bird herself. All too soon the strident ring of her alarm ensured she was fully awake. Stretching, she got out of bed and pulled back the curtains. The day had promise—it wasn't raining—and she had a lot to get done. Showered and dressed, she quickly made a cafetière and prepared her fruit and cereal. Taking it to the breakfast bar she found her notebook with her lists, casting her eye over them to remind herself of everything she needed to find out about the *Granny Fi* series, and the Little Bear company too.

A brisk walk brought her once again to the revolving doors of Little Bear, where the same receptionist was on duty. 'Hi, it's Sam, isn't it?' smiled the receptionist.

Sam nodded, 'Hi.'

'How did your first day go?' asked the receptionist.

'It went really quickly—lots to learn and think about. Thanks for asking … Debbie,' added Sam, noticing Debbie's name badge.

Debbie smiled. 'Well, I hope day two goes just as well. You know your way up now?'

'Yes, thanks—it's a bit of a labyrinth but I think I'll be OK!'

Climbing the stairs to the first floor, Sam spotted the workstation she'd used yesterday, and started to sort out her laptop, ready for the day ahead.

'Hi, Jen' she called, pleased to recognise Jen's head of wavy hair above the workstation partition.

'Oh, Sam, hi. How did you get on yesterday? I didn't see you after your meeting with Melissa—I was in other meetings all day. How did it go?'

'Shall we get a coffee, and I'll fill you in,' offered Sam.

The two women walked over to the kitchen area, which had the basics for making hot drinks. 'It's not exactly the best coffee in town …' Jen said apologetically, spooning instant coffee into mugs.

'No, it's not,' laughed Sam. 'Perhaps we could go out at lunchtime and find something nicer?'

'Good idea,' said Jen. 'There's a great coffee shop just round the corner—Gino's. Do you know it?'

'No,' said Sam. 'I'm new to this area so I'll go with your recommendation.'

'I think you'll like it,' said Jen, stirring in the floating grains of instant coffee with a pained expression. 'So, what about the meeting—what did you make of Melissa?'

'She was not impressed with the *Granny Fi* sales, and she wanted to know what's in the marketing plan. I explained I'd only just joined but both she and Brendan are really pushing me, so I've got a lot to do—you did warn me!'

'Hmm, I'm not surprised. *Granny Fi* sales have been wobbly for a little while now. I get the feeling Brendan wants to get rid of the series—and maybe even Melissa, but I may be wrong.'

'He did say he thought *Granny Fi* had had her day, which didn't go down well with Melissa. It was a bit of a shock to hear that, as I thought the series was a big part of my job. I need to ask Brendan about it.'

Chapter Two

'Melissa must have been furious,' grinned Jen. 'Let's talk more at lunch time—I can fill you in on Melissa and Brendan then.'

Back at her workstation, Sam felt pleased that she seemed to have made one friend at Little Bear. She logged in to her laptop so she could message a few people she wanted to talk to: the editor for the series, the sales manager, the designer ... and, of course, her manager, Brendan. As other people started their working day, messages were returned to fix times to meet. Melissa might believe that *Granny Fi* could not exist without her, but it was very clear there was a whole team behind the series at Little Bear.

'Where will I find Tony Pearson?' she enquired, hoping someone in the open office would reply. A man with a ponytail looked up 'next floor, first on the right.'

'*I wonder what Tony's take is going to be on Granny Fi sales,*' Sam mused as she climbed the stairs with their well-worn carpet. If there had been a pattern it was now heavily disguised by the hundreds of shoes that had walked on it over many years.

Finding a door with the name 'Tony Pearson' on it she knocked, and hearing a brusque 'enter' she opened the door and went in.

'Morning—ah, you must be Sam. Excuse the mess. Here, let me move these and you can have a seat.'

'Thanks for agreeing to meet.' Sam smiled as she spoke, glancing quickly at the numerous piles of books, proofs, and other print outs. Tony's face was just about visible behind the piled-up paperwork on his desk, although he didn't look as though he usually sat for long. Restlessly moving one pile of papers to another, and then to another, he was constantly on the move, standing up again before perching back on the edge of his chair and smoothing down his dishevelled hair.

'Well, what can I do for you?' asked Tony as he fiddled with his pen.

Taking a deep breath, Sam explained. 'I started this week as the Marketing Manager for children's books, which really means the

Granny Fi series. As far as I can work out, *Granny Fi* has been the cash cow for the business for some time and although we publish plenty of other books, nothing has succeeded as *Granny Fi* did.'

'*Did*?' queried Tony, one eyebrow raised quizzically as he looked across at Sam. 'You make it sound as though *Granny Fi* is history.'

'If the sales figures I saw yesterday are right, then *Granny Fi* is in trouble. The sales must have been fantastic for years, but more recently they look a bit up and down. And now—well, over the last six months since the new book came out—it's not looking good at all,' Sam explained, thinking back to the sales graph she'd seen yesterday. 'What do you think is happening, and what are your thoughts on how we get *Granny Fi* selling again?'

'You'll have met Melissa, I take it?' asked Tony, looking directly at her for the first time since Sam had entered his office.

'I did, and she wasn't happy about the sales at all. She wants a relaunch with a new illustrator, and she wants to see the marketing plan. But I can't come up with that until I understand the series better.'

'Hmm,' mused Tony. 'No surprises there. That's what she always says when sales take a dip. I had a devil of a job getting that latest book—what was it now? Oh yes, *Granny Fi and the Poorly Bee*. Couldn't get it into bookshops at all.' Tony sighed and shifted uneasily in his seat.

'Why didn't they want to take the book? Melissa said that a new book always got good sales and lifted the sales of the whole series, because the new one attracts new customers who then came back for more.'

'That's what used to happen, but Melissa doesn't appreciate how the book world is changing. That's why the sales figures you saw yesterday are showing such a downturn, compared with even just a couple of years ago.'

'Brendan said much the same. Buying habits are changing, it seems.'

'Yes, it doesn't look as though the latest story will match the sales of previous new *Granny Fi* books. By the way, where did you work before you came here? I assume you know the book trade, or publishing?'

'Not really. I've always worked in marketing but not in publishing. I realise there's a lot to learn …'

'Huh' snorted Tony, 'you've no idea just how much!'

'That's where I need to gain from your experience,' said Sam, keeping her tone neutral. 'Why is *Granny Fi* out of favour?'

'It's the kids. The parents remember *Granny Fi* and want to read the books to their kids, but then they find the little darlings don't like them—*Granny Fi's* old-fashioned, and the last lot of illustrations didn't help. Kaye—she's the illustrator—said at the time that she struggled to draw bees. So going with a story all about bees wasn't the best idea, but Melissa was set on it for some reason. We need something up to date, about the sort of things kids want to learn about now—you know, all the stuff they learn in schools. Climate. Gender. Not picnics and scooters. Or bees.'

Is that what the bookshops say?' queried Sam.

'Not in so many words, but if they can't move the books off the shelves, they won't want to take more. Draw your own conclusions,' replied Tony with a dismissive shrug of his shoulders.

'Hmm, I'd like to have a bit more to go on than just assumptions. Can you give me the details of some of your bookshop contacts so I can speak to them?'

'I can …. I'll email you the details for one of our long-standing bookshop buyers. But be careful. We don't want him putting two and two together and reading more into this.'

'What do you mean?' asked Sam.

'We don't want them thinking Little Bear is struggling,' he explained. 'We need them to feel confident so we can get our other books on the shelves. There's more to Little Bear than *Granny Fi*.'

'Yeah, I get it,' said Sam. 'I'll be careful. And thanks. I'll let you know if I find out anything interesting. Oh, by the way, how well do you know Kaye? What's she like?'

'No one sees Kaye. She keeps herself to herself in her little corner of Cumbria. Everything has to be done by snail mail or phone. She won't come here for meetings.'

'How does she work with Melissa then,' asked Sam.

'How does anyone work with Melissa!' Tony grinned unexpectedly. 'If you want to know about Kaye, ask Jason—the designer,' he added.

'Oh yes, he was in the meeting with Melissa and Brendan yesterday. Thanks, I'll do that,' Sam said as she got up to leave.

How patronising! Sam muttered on her way down the stairs.

'I'm sorry?'

'Oh, was I talking to myself? Hi, I'm Sam. Hey, you're Jason, aren't you?'

'Yes, and yes! We were in the same meeting—with Melissa and Brendan,' grinned Jason, looking much more relaxed than he had yesterday.

'I'm not likely to forget that one. What a start to my first day!' laughed Sam. 'Have you got a few minutes? I'd love to find out a bit more about the *Granny Fi* illustrator and Tony thought you probably know her best.'

'I wouldn't say I really know her—she's a very private person. But I have worked with her for quite a few years. My desk is downstairs, if you want to follow me. I've got a few minutes before my next meeting.'

'Thanks, appreciate it,' said Sam. Jason moved quickly down the stairs and round the winding corridor to a room that was full of light. 'Oh, this is nice.'

'Yes, one of the best spaces in the building. I need it for working on illustrations and design,' explained Jason.

'Mmm. How long have you worked on the *Granny Fi* books?'

'Since I started here, around ten years ago. I do other stuff too—the one-off books, and other series.'

'What do you make of it all? I mean, those sales figures we saw yesterday looked … well, dire,' ventured Sam.

'I know. I knew the new book would bomb. The illustrations weren't up to Kaye's usual standard, and it was a weak story. But Melissa insisted we went ahead. It was timely, according to her.'

'What did she mean by that?'

'Oh, it was about saving a bee, which she said is 'on topic' at the moment,' explained Jason, using his fingers to indicate the quote marks.

'I've read it. I thought it was a nice story. And my friend's little girl liked it.'

'Nice doesn't sell. Kids today—well, most kids—want something a bit more edgy. Or funny. Not a twee old lady giving sugary water to a bee.'

'Oh. And what about the rest of the books?'

Jason sighed. 'It's not looking great to be honest. We're so reliant on *Granny Fi*, but with Melissa stuck in the past, and Kaye keeping herself out of the way, it's hard to bring the books into the 21st century—and that's another problem, they're all books. Printed ones, nothing digital.'

'You could do some really fun stuff if the books were digital and interactive. And I noticed there's no social media for anything that Little Bear publishes. I was hoping I could change that.'

'Good luck,' grinned Jason. 'Brendan's not interested. He doesn't get social media so he assumes it's irrelevant. And as for getting books digitised … well, that would mean investment and I can't see Brendan going for that. Sorry, but I've got to get on with some work now,' said Jason, glancing at his computer screen.

'Of course. Thanks a lot for your time. See you around,' said Sam

---

Sam slipped behind her desk, and logged into her laptop. Five minutes until her meeting with Brendan. She checked the list of questions she'd jotted down yesterday evening, and added a few more after her meetings with Tony and Jason. The biggest question of all was: was there really a job here for her, if *Granny Fi* sales were so dismal?

A short walk along the upstairs corridor brought her to another door with Brendan's name on it. She tapped firmly, and entered. 'Hi, I've got a meeting with Brendan,' she explained to the tired-looking woman behind the desk.

'And you are?' the woman asked, her tone suggesting a lack of curiosity.

'Sam, Sam Holliday. I'm new. I've just joined as Marketing Manager.'

The woman sniffed. 'Very nice, I'm sure.' She put down a framed photograph she had been looking at to pick up her phone. After a few seconds a voice at the other end snapped 'yes?' There was a short exchange.

'You're to go in,' the woman said in her lacklustre voice.

'Thanks,' replied Sam, pushing open the inner door to reveal a large room with shelving from floor to ceiling. She glanced briefly around the room thinking it would be impossible to find a space for another book on any of the shelves, which was probably why so many were piled on the floor and every other available space.

'Well don't just stand there, come in and find somewhere to sit,' commanded Brendan. 'Fran, isn't it?'

'No, Sam. Sam Holliday. I joined yesterday, and I was in the meeting with you and Melissa,' she reminded him, moving a pile of papers onto the floor so she could sit on a chair.

'Yes, I know that. I may be older than you but I'm not quite senile. You're going to give us the marketing plan to get Melissa's little books selling again.'

'I hope so …'

'Hope?' queried Brendan, a flush spreading over his already florid cheeks. '*Hope* won't get the job done. We need a solid marketing plan. That's what I've employed you to do.'

'I understand that, and I will produce a plan. But …'

'Let me make myself very clear,' he said, emphasising each word with a jab of his finger. 'You produce the plan by next Friday or you needn't bother with the rest of your probationary period.'

'Oh!' Sam cleared her throat and spoke more firmly than she felt. 'I need more information before I can do that.'

Chapter Two

'You've got the sales figures. What else do you need?'

'I'd like to look at the sales information more closely. And I need to talk to some booksellers. Ideally to parents and kids but I can't do that for next Friday. I need to talk to Melissa, and to Kaye. And people here—I've already spoken to Tony and Jason, but I want to talk to my colleague in marketing and to editorial as well.'

'You're going to be busy then, aren't you? Best you get on with it,' said Brendan, waving his hand at her as though she was a rather irritating fly.

'Right, yes, I will. So, you're OK with me going to meet Kaye in her home if that's the only way I can get to talk to her?'

'I've no idea why you want to talk to the eccentric old bat, but go if you must.'

'Thanks,' said Sam, and got up to leave. Once through the door and the outer office, she breathed out and muttered *eccentric old bat indeed. What century does he think he's in?*

'Ready for lunch?' asked a voice.

'Oh Jen, great timing—let's go!' said Sam.

'Sounds as though you need to escape,' grinned Jen.

'You could say that!' Sam agreed.

'Gino's OK with you? There is another café, but I think Gino's has the best coffee.'

'Gino's it is then,' smiled Sam as she put on her coat and scarf.

It was a short walk to Gino's. It was, Jen explained, the most popular of Lower Rushford's cafés, perhaps because it was conveniently close to other shops in the High Street. Opening the door to the café, a wave of warmth and a smell of freshly ground coffee greeted Sam and Jen as they stepped inside, out of the cold, January day. A couple of people were quietly busy on their laptops, while a low buzz of conversation came from tables with couples having lunch.

'*Buon giorno*! Come in, come in. A table for two? You like the window? *Si*?'

'Er, no, we'd prefer a table away from the window, please,' said Sam, thinking she didn't want to be seen by any passing Little Bear staff.

'No problem. Here, this is good for you?' asked the obliging waiter, pulling out chairs and collecting menus for the two women. 'Something to drink, perhaps?'

'What would you like?' Jen asked Sam.

'A double espresso for me.'

'A latte for me, please,' added Jen.

'*Grazie*. And I can recommend the fettucine with chicken and mushrooms. Or, the pizza oven is hot so perhaps a pizza lunch?' the waiter suggested.

'Would you mind coming back in a couple of minutes? We just need coffee for now,' said Sam, sounding decidedly caffeine-deprived.

'*Certo*. Coffee will be with you very soon!'

Sam settled into her seat with a heavy sigh. 'Gosh,' said Jen, taking in Sam's worried face, 'maybe we should go for the pasta. It's the best comfort food I know, and it sounds as though you need it!'

'Oh dear,' Sam sighed again. 'I'm all right really, although it has been quite a morning!'

'What's up?'

'Meetings. One with Tony, an impromptu one with Jason, and another with Gordon.'

'Gordon? I can't think of anyone called Gordon.'

Sam grinned mischievously. 'I've re-named Brendan. Well, not to his face. He can't remember my name. So far, he's called me Pam or Fran, never Sam. So I'm calling him Gordon No Manners. I think it suits him better than Brendan McManners.'

'Ouch!' Jen grinned back at her. 'He really has got to you—and yesterday you said you thought he seemed nice! I knew it would only be a matter of time before you changed your mind, but one day for a complete u-turn is going some!'

'I know. He's told me that I've got to come up with a marketing plan for the *Granny Fi* series by next Friday, or basically I'm fired,' explained Sam, looking glum. 'I can't afford to lose this job. I've just bought a house, and the mortgage is—well, quite a commitment.'

'Jumping jellybeans,' exclaimed Jen 'oh, excuse the language,' she said as she saw Sam's quizzical expression. 'It's something we always said at home—my parents had a strict no-swearing rule. But really, Brendan—OK, Gordon—has really gone too far this time. He can't just sack you!'

'Probably not, and although I could kick up a lot of fuss if he did, I just want to keep my job. I've got a mortgage to pay!'

The waiter returned with their coffees, and conversation paused as they looked appreciatively at their drinks.

'This is just what I need,' said Sam.

'What did you do before you took this job? Were you in publishing?' asked Jen.

'No. Actually, I worked for the police force.'

'What! You could get one of your mates to arrest Brendan if he sacks you!' said Jen with a gleeful note in her voice.

Sam chuckled. 'Hmm. I worked in marketing, not as a policewoman.'

'I can't imagine how you'd go about marketing a police force,' said Jen, looking momentarily thoughtful.

'There was lots of social media going on—completely different to Little Bear.'

'I don't think you can mention Little Bear and social media in the same breath. Little Bear does catalogues, posters, and bookshop displays. Brendan doesn't understand social media so he won't let us use it for marketing. In fact, I'm not sure he really understands marketing at all.'

'Brendan seems to decide everything. I report to him. How about you, and the rest of the staff?' Sam asked.

'Yep, Brendan keeps both hands firmly on the reins. Most of us report to him. It's not a big company—around 20 or so staff. Marketing is small. There's you, me, and the designers work on publicity as well as the books. And then there's a few editorial people, a production manager, a finance person, and then other stuff just gets off-loaded onto whoever Brendan wants to do it. Like HR.

Out of the twenty or so who work there, I'd say around fifteen report to Brendan. You must have met most people on your first day!'

'The size was part of the appeal. The police force was just too big, and too impersonal. I wanted to get stuck into something—well, something I believe in. Sorry if this sounds a bit pretentious, but I wanted to work somewhere I could make a difference, rather than being just a cog in the wheel. I used to read the *Granny Fi* stories to my friend's daughter when she was little. We really liked them,' Sam added with a hint of wistfulness.

'Don't write *Granny Fi* off just yet. And there's plenty of other good books. It's not all *Granny Fi*.' Jen paused, then asked 'Where did you move from?'

'Kidlington. My partner was in the police force. He's a sergeant. We split up, and I decided to make a clean break: new job, new house, new town. No new man though.'

'Wow, that was brave! Had you been together long?'

'Brave or stupid—time will tell! We were together for about five years.' Sam looked away, gathering her thoughts. The waiter returned, and both women ordered the fettucine.

Jen talked about her work at Little Bear before Sam said 'Tell me, what's going on with the *Granny Fi* series? Tony said he couldn't get bookshops to take the latest book, which according to him should never have seen the light of day. Jason wasn't that positive either. Is the series really in its death throws? And what's that going to mean for Little Bear if it is? Melissa seemed to think that if *Granny Fi* sinks, so does the business. Sorry, too many questions!'

'No, it's fine. I'm just not sure where to start really .... Oh, look, here's our lunch.'

'Here you are, ladies,' said the waiter as he put two plates of steaming pasta in front of Jen and Sam with a flourish. 'Some *parmigiano? Non? Buon appetito!*'

'This looks good!, said Sam, picking up her fork and giving the pasta a stir. 'Mmm, it smells delicious too. I could get used to this!'

'It's great, isn't it, and not too expensive—for a treat, I mean,' said Jen.

Chapter Two

'I don't think either my bank account or my waistline could cope with this too often!' grinned Sam.

'You're in better shape than me, but I know what you mean!'

'It's only walking that keeps the weight off. I eat like a horse but I usually walk a lot at weekends to keep a bit fit. I thought I might join a local walking group. Get to know a few people.'

'Mmm, good idea. Not my thing, but I bet there is a group. There's a town website so you might find something on there.'

The two women fell quiet as they tucked into their meal. Around them, the hum of conversation continued as more people came in, looking for a table.

'Getting back to your questions,' Jen said, 'I can't work out what's going on at the moment. About a year ago the company was doing really well. We had a pay rise, there was talk of doing up some of the office space, although that didn't actually happen. We've always relied too much on *Granny Fi* but the books were doing so well, and we knew there was another one coming out this year. And then suddenly, it's all gloom and doom.'

'That's weird,' said Sam. 'Who's the finance manager? I wanted to have a really good look at the sales figures for myself, so I need to speak to them.'

'Clive Frobisher.' Jen's nose wrinkled slightly. 'He's one of the directors. He's Brendan's cousin. Brendan's mother and aunt—his aunt is Kaye Butterworth—started the business originally. Tony's another cousin, and he and Clive are on the board with Brendan, and Kaye. His mother isn't actively involved these days although she is still on the Board officially.'

'Kaye Butterworth, the illustrator, you mean?' Sam was surprised.

'Yeah, she and Brendan's mother started the company back in—oh, gosh, the 1980s, I think.'

'No wonder Brendan's desperate for the marketing plan. He wouldn't want his family's business to fold, would he?'

'Wouldn't he? I wouldn't trust Brendan as far as I could throw him.' There was a pause as both women tried to imagine throwing

Brendan any distance. Catching each other's eye, they started to giggle.

'Hey, wait a minute' Jen said, pushing her plate away and getting a pen out of her bag. Drawing rapidly on her paper napkin, she turned it round to show Sam who immediately burst out laughing.

'Jen, that's genius! You've got him exactly! You're so clever!'

The drawing showed Brendan, looking furious and amazed, with Jen hurling him across his office, papers flying everywhere.

'Aw, thanks. I've always liked doing drawings, especially when they make people laugh.'

'Do you do any book illustrations? Like graphic novels?'

'Only cartoons for fun, or for friends. Little Bear doesn't publish the right sort of books for my type of work.'

'Perhaps Brendan should think about it though. Graphic novels have really taken off now. You see them everywhere!'

'True. Don't think Brendan's noticed though.' Jen grinned suddenly. 'Can I be there when you put the idea to him?'

'Ha, ha, I might save that for after the marketing plan,' said Sam.

'Good thinking. And talking of plans, what are you up to this afternoon?'

'I'm meeting Stacey Barber—you know, the production manager, at half two. I'll give Clive a call, and maybe the bookshop guy Tony said I could talk to. I'll have to contact Kaye at some point to see if I can meet her.'

'Best we get moving then,' said Jen, waving for the bill. 'No, no, my treat. Think of it as my way of saying welcome.'

'Oh, that's really kind of you, Jen. Thanks. Much needed! Don't forget your drawing.'

'Thanks. It's not one I'd want just anyone to see!'

'It is funny though—unless you're Brendan, of course!' said Sam.

Wrapping themselves in coats and scarves, the two women stepped back out into the cold to walk back to the office.

Chapter Two

On the top floor of the Little Bear offices, Tony slipped into Brendan's office. Brendan's secretary was at lunch.

'How do you keep track of all this paperwork, Brendan?' asked Tony as he moved a pile of paper from one of the scuffed leather chairs to the floor.

'You're a fine one to talk! Careful with those. Don't muddle them up. I know exactly what they are,' said Brendan.

'If you say so!' Tony looked up as the door opened. 'Oh, Clive, here you are. Good luck with finding somewhere to sit.'

'Stop fussing, Tony. Clive, just put that pile there on the floor. No, not there, the other side. Right, we haven't got long.'

'So, what's up?' asked Clive, polishing his glasses as he always did when nervous.

'That new marketing woman. That's what's up,' said Tony.

'Exactly. Pam, Fran … never can remember the wretched woman's name'

'It's Sam. You appointed her, remember?' said Tony.

'I know. I thought she'd do some fluffy bit of marketing that would keep Melissa happy, but she's only been here two days and she's already asking too many questions. I'm worried.'

'I've fobbed her off as much as I can,' said Tony. 'I met her this morning and told her the last *Granny Fi* book was unsaleable. She wanted to speak to a bookshop so I gave her old Norman's number —he's never been a *Granny Fi* fan so he'll just confirm what I told her.'

'Good. Clive, has she spoken to you yet?'

'No, but it won't be long. I can bluff a bit saying the accounts are being audited, or that the system is down and I can't run sales reports. With a bit of luck, she'll get bored, or forget.'

'Hmm. She did say she wanted to meet with Kaye, so she'll be away for a couple of days which gives us a bit more time.'

'How long have we got until we see a contract?' asked Tony.

'I don't think it will be long now. They want to move fast so I think everything will need to be wrapped up by the end of the month if they do want to partner with us. And before you ask, Clive, whatever date we're given, it'll be non-negotiable so you'll have to get that legal company you've appointed to speed up,' said Brendan, getting up and hitching his tangerine-coloured corduroy trousers more comfortably over his paunch. The meeting was over.

Sam settled into a chair in Stacey Barber's neat and tidy office. While there were a lot of books, and some piles of proofs, everything looked organised in sharp contrast to Tony and Brendan's chaotic offices. The woman sitting behind the desk was as neat as her office. With her no-nonsense straight dark hair, smart top and pendant she would have looked severe if it wasn't for the over-sized purple-framed glasses and coordinating earrings.

'It's good to meet you, Sam, and it's great to have another person in marketing. Jen's been really stretched for the last few weeks. What do you make of it all so far?'

'I'm not sure, to be completely honest. I'm curious about this downturn in sales for the *Granny Fi* series, and I'm trying to find out more about the last book. It hasn't sold at all. What's your take on it, Stacey?'

Stacey hesitated before speaking. 'You know I've only been here a couple of months?'

Sam shook her head, looking puzzled.

'Yes, the person who was in this role before me was a Production Director, and was on the Board. I got taken on as Production Manager. I was at Bowland Press before.'

'Why did the Director leave?'

'Well, he didn't leave in the sense you mean. He died.'

'Died? Of natural causes?'

'Yes, natural causes. What were you expecting? Murder?' Stacey said, laughing.

'No, well, yes, I mean, I didn't know what to think.'

'Ah, sorry. There's no mystery though. Frank McManners had a heart attack at the top of the stairs.'

'You mean the stairs in this building, or at home?'

'Here. His body was found by Brendan's secretary. He'd fallen headlong, from the first to the ground floor. Poor Enid, she was in shock for days.'

'I can imagine. Enid—that's the woman who's in the office just outside Brendan's. She's his secretary?'

'Yes, that's right,' said Stacey.

'I met her this morning. I thought she was a bit miserable.'

'I don't think she's really got over it. Think about it, every time she comes into work and goes upstairs to her office, she must see that scene all over again. A sort of gruesome groundhog day.'

'Hmm, I see what you mean. So, Frank McManners. What relation was he to Brendan? I hear the Board are all family members.'

'Yes, he was Brendan's brother.'

'Oh! Tough for Brendan.'

'Tougher for Frank. The two never got on. Always plenty of sparks flying in the Board meetings, especially just before Frank died. The office they use for their meetings is just above mine so I could hear the shouting—and they shouted quite a bit.'

'Brendan's got quite a booming voice even when he's talking normally!'

'Yes, he's a forceful character, but he's been all right with me, so far. I'm waiting for him to get back to me with some information on who printed the latest *Granny Fi* book. I can't find the stock.'

'Really? I thought it would all be in a warehouse somewhere. Tony said he couldn't get bookshops to take it. But if there's no stock, the bookshops couldn't get copies anyway.'

'Oh? I didn't know about that. The printing's done in China as the costs are much lower, even with the shipping. It's all been a bit erratic with Covid and lockdowns. But other books have been getting through for a while now, except *Granny Fi and the Poorly Bee*. I haven't seen an invoice yet either. Brendan said he'd look into it.

'I'm going to be speaking to Clive soon, so I'll see if he knows anything. I'll let you know what he says.

'Thanks. Apparently, Frank wasn't always on top of the paperwork. Or that's what Brendan told me.'

'If Frank's office was anything like Brendan's or Tony's the paperwork was probably on top of him!'

'Good point,' laughed Stacey. 'Let me know if you get anywhere with the invoice.'

Back at her desk, Sam decided her next task was to call Kaye. The phone rang and rang, but eventually a quiet yet firm voice answered 'Kaye Butterworth.'

'Hello, Miss Butterworth. You won't know me, but my name's Sam Holliday and I've recently joined Little Bear. I'll be handling the marketing for the *Granny Fi* series.'

'So, he finally got round to appointing someone, did he?'

'Er, I'm not sure what you mean.'

'My nephew. Melissa demanded he got someone in to do the marketing. The other woman left. It was all rather abrupt.'

'Ah, I didn't know that. I met Melissa yesterday and I know she wants to see the marketing plan.'

'Good luck with that then.'

Quickly, Sam said 'I'm hoping you can help.'

'Help? I don't know anything about marketing.'

'But you do know a lot about the series. And I can't put a plan together until I know the books better. I'd really like to find out more about the illustrations.'

'Well.' There was a pause. Sam held her breath. 'Well,' Kaye continued. 'You're the first person to take any interest in those.'

'Really? They're so important! It would be great to have time to talk to you.'

'I'm not coming to Lower Rushford. If you want to talk, you'll have come here. There's a pub in the village that does accommodation.'

'That would be fantastic!'

'No need to gush. Now, when are you thinking of coming here?'

'I'll need to check with the pub, but how about I try to get booked in for Thursday, so we can meet on Friday?'

'This Thursday? You *are* keen.'

'Brendan wants the marketing plan by end of next week …'

'Well, best you start packing then. I'll expect you here at 2pm on Friday. Bring plenty of layers. It's cold.'

'Will do, and thank you! It will be …'

'A useful meeting, I hope,' said Kaye, dryly.

'Indeed,' said Sam, disconnecting the call. *Phew*, she thought. *What on earth have I let myself in for?*

Frowning, Kaye Butterworth replaced her phone's receiver and sighed. It was the second call from Little Bear in one day, and in Kaye's opinion, that was at least one too many. The marketing woman sounded pleasant enough, if inclined to unnecessary enthusiasm but perhaps that's how you had to be to work in marketing. At least she was interested enough in the books to want to understand them better. Full marks for her enthusiasm there.

No marks though to her nephew, Brendan. What was he thinking of, calling to see if she'd thought any more about publishing in China. Surely she had made it perfectly clear that she was not going to re-draw Granny Fi just to make more money. Everyone had done very well on the sales of the *Granny Fi* series for many years. Changing Granny Fi simply felt wrong, and a change of heart was definitely not on the cards. Brendan would simply have to accept it. He'd bulldozered enough of his ideas through over the years. But not this time.

Sam checked her phone. Two texts. One from the pub confirming her room booking, and the other from her mother asking how day two had gone. How had it gone? She felt she had made a friend, but on the work front she still had more questions than answers. But she wasn't going to tell her mother that so she sent a cheery reply saying she was off to Cumbria on Thursday to meet with the illustrator.

'Exciting,' messaged her mother, adding several variations of smiley emojis.

Sam replied with a thumbs up, and checked her email. Confirmation of her train ticket to Penrith, and confirmation of her taxi to Upper Braithwaite, the village where Kaye lived. It had all fallen into place so easily.

'*Tomorrow, I'd better talk to Clive and to that book buyer.*' She cast her eye over her list, and although there was still a lot to do, she felt she had made some progress.

Sam went into the kitchen, and started to prepare her meal. Chopping vegetables was soothing, and the questions that had been whirring around her head settled as the heap of peppers, onions, and mushrooms grew. A glass of wine, and supper on a tray while watching the latest episode of her favourite crime drama made a good way to end her day.

Flicking through her phone before she went to bed, she remembered Jen telling her about the Lower Rushford website. She soon found it, and yes, there were a couple of local walking groups. One sounded promising. It was for working walkers looking for a good walk at weekends, involving a stop at a pub along the way. She quickly emailed the walk leader before heading for bed.

Chapter Three

Wednesday, January 19th

Morning came all too soon, and with a chilly breeze at her back Sam set a brisk pace to the office. Exiting the revolving door into the reception area, Sam was surprised to see a number of people gathered there, including Brendan.

He was looking up at the logo above the reception desk, hands on hips, and red in the face. 'Vandals! How dare they! It's an outrage!'

Debbie, the receptionist, looked close to tears. 'I don't know, I just don't know,' she said, but Brendan paid her no attention.

Everyone else was looking at the wall behind Debbie's desk. They all looked baffled, and some were looking upset. Sam stepped forward to take a closer look. The Little Bear logo—the silhouette of a small bear—had an ugly red cross crudely painted on it, and a knife was impaled into the wall, running through the bear's body. Under the point of the knife was a piece of paper with something drawn on it.

'You—get that knife out of there,' barked Brendan to a tall young man. Sam realised it was Jason.

'Er, I don't think that's a good idea,' said Jason.

'I'm telling you to get the damned knife out of the wall. Do it!'

'It might have fingerprints on it. Are you going to call the police? It looks like a threat. I don't think we should touch it.'

One or two people shuddered and turned away.

'A threat? It's an insult! Yes, call the police. You, whatever your name is, get on to them now,' demanded Brendan.

'Yes,' said Debbie, looking flustered. 'Should I call 999?'

'There's no need to be melodramatic. Nobody's died—yet. Although has anyone checked the offices? No? Right, I'll do that.' Brendan walked purposefully up the stairs while his staff waited, uncertain where they should go. A few minutes passed while Debbie found the number to call to report the incident.

While she was waiting for the all-clear from Brendan, Sam looked more closely at the paper under the knife. A horrible thought came to her. It was a drawing. A drawing like the one she'd seen Jen draw yesterday.

'OK, no bodies,' said Brendan. 'Have you got hold of the police yet?'

'Yes,' said Debbie. 'Someone will be over later this morning to take a look. We're not to touch anything until they get here.'

'The rest of you had better get on with your work. You—my office, now.'

Debbie, looking nervous and upset, followed Brendan upstairs to his office.

'Debbie,' Sam called. 'I'll make some tea for you for after you've talked to Brendan.'

Debbie turned on the stairs. 'Thanks, Sam. That would be good.'

Sam, and the other members of staff including Jason, moved off to their offices. Jason gave her a quick smile. 'What a start to the day!' he commented.

'Yes. Why would anyone do that?' asked Sam.

'No idea. And *when* did they do it?' asked Jason.

'It's not something you'd notice on the way out—only when you come in to the office, so it could have been done last night.'

Chapter Three

'Oh, we'll all have to account for ourselves now, won't we,' said Jason, shoulders sagging at the thought.

Sam groaned. 'I had so much I wanted to get done this morning.'

Jason smiled ruefully. 'Yes, same here. Well, I suppose I'd better get to my desk.'

Sam went upstairs, and was switching on her laptop as Jen came in.

'Hi Jen, have you heard what's happened?'

'No, what?'

'The logo on the wall in reception's been vandalised.'

'How do you mean—vandalised?'

'Someone's painted a red cross on the bear, and stuck a knife in it. And there's a piece of paper underneath the knife.'

'Is there anything on the paper?'

'We don't know. We can't touch anything until the police get here. But, oh, Jen, it looks like a drawing. One of your drawings.'

'No!' Jen's face paled, and she sat down abruptly. She looked as though she might be sick.

'I'm really sorry, I should have broken it to you more gently. I might be wrong.'

Jen turned to her desk, opened the drawers, and rummaged through some papers. 'Oh!' said Jen, clamping her hand over her mouth. 'They've gone!'

'What's gone?' asked Sam.

'I had quite a few sketches—sort-of caricatures of some of the people who work here. Nothing nasty, just a bit of fun. I've done a few of Brendan but those ones have all disappeared!'

'Oh, Jen, that's terrible,' said Sam. 'Come on, I said I'd make Debbie some tea. Brendan's hauled her off to his office. She's going to need some TLC when she gets out. And so do you.'

The kettle had just boiled as Debbie appeared, looking tearful.

'Debbie, tea or coffee? Sorry there's nothing stronger. Did Brendan give you a hard time?'

Debbie sniffed. 'Tea, please. He more or less said it was all my fault! He said I must have been away from my desk for ages to give someone time to do all that, but honestly, I only nipped to the loo a couple of times.'

'Come on, let's go back to my desk. Grab yourselves a chair, and then we can talk,' said Sam as she finished making the drinks.

'I've got some emergency chocolate biscuits somewhere,' said Jen.

'Well, this definitely qualifies as an emergency, so dig them out!' Sam said as cheerfully as she could.

The three women pulled up chairs around Sam's desk, and waited while Jen rummaged for the biscuits.

'You must have seen it as you came through the entrance door this morning, I suppose?' Sam asked.

'No, I didn't. I came in, took my coat off, and got settled in behind my desk. I didn't look at the wall. Not until Brendan came in. He noticed it straightaway, and went ballistic. I couldn't understand what he was on about. You know how he gets. He was bright red, jabbing his finger at the wall, and spluttering. And then I turned round, which is when I saw it.' Debbie shuddered. 'It's horrible.'

'Ah, here's the biscuits. Go on, Debbie, you need the sugar,' said Jen. There was a pause as they all munched thoughtfully, oblivious of the crumbs.

'That feels a bit better,' said Debbie. 'Thanks for doing this.'

'Did you see what's on the paper?' Jen asked anxiously.

'Not really, it's a drawing, I think,' Debbie said.

'Who do you think could have done it—and when?' asked Sam.

'I think it must have been after I went home. I leave at 5. A few other people left just before me, but there were still others around. Brendan's the last to leave, usually.'

'Quite a list of suspects then. You were at your desk when I left,' said Jen.

'And I left when you did, Debbie. Do you remember, I followed you out the door?'

'Yes, you did. You two are off the hook then.'

Sam and Jen exchanged glances.

'Not entirely,' said Jen. 'You see, it sounds as though the piece of paper might belong to me.'

'What?' Debbie looked startled.

'I do drawings. Caricatures really, and I had a few in my drawer. They've gone, and Sam thinks the drawing on the wall is in the same style as mine. I drew one for her yesterday, so she knows the sort of thing I do.'

'Who knew about your drawings, apart from me?' Sam asked.

'A few people, I suppose. Not Brendan, obviously. Or any of the Board. But Stacey knows, Jason in Design, Amy in editorial, Enid...'

'I can't see one of them doing this. It has to be someone who was looking through people's desks, hoping to find some money or something, and they found your drawings,' said Sam.

'Sounds a bit unlikely though, doesn't it?' said Jen.

'About as unlikely as stabbing a logo with a knife. I mean, what's it all about?' Neither Jen nor Debbie could answer Sam's question, and both looked troubled.

'I'd better get back downstairs for when the police arrive,' said Debbie, getting up to go. 'Thanks for the tea and biscuits.'

'We'd better get on too, I suppose. Not sure I can concentrate at the moment though,' said Jen.

'Why don't you show me what you've been working on—for *Granny Fi*, or the other books?' suggested Sam. 'I'd really like to see that.'

'Good idea. Give me a few minutes and I'll get everything ready for you.'

It was difficult to concentrate after the morning's events, but Sam tried to keep herself busy, preparing for her meeting with Kaye and thinking about the other people she needed to speak to. Before long,

Jen appeared at Sam's desk saying she was ready to talk her through the marketing materials and campaigns, and the morning went surprisingly quickly as they looked through catalogues, and point of sale publicity for bookshops.

'Did any booksellers actually order the publicity for the new *Granny Fi* story?' asked Sam, looking at a shelf wobbler with a picture of a smiling Granny Fi. There was a curious-looking bee buzzing over Granny Fi's head. The artwork was quite nicely drawn (although the bee was rather small), but perhaps it did look a little old-fashioned.

'No, and I didn't really think about that until this week. It's been so busy since the other marketing person left. I wasn't working on *Granny Fi* before, and I didn't have time to check through what publicity had gone where.'

'Don't feel bad about it,' said Sam. 'I get it. Why did the other marketing person leave?'

'I'm not sure. It was all hushed up. One day she was here, and the next day I was told she wouldn't be back.'

'Oh, that doesn't sound good,' Sam said, looking thoughtful. 'Did you see her again, after she'd left, I mean?'

Jen shook her head. 'We didn't really socialise outside of work so when she left, she just disappeared.'

'But she'd produced all the publicity for the new book—and for other books too. She can't have been sacked for not doing her job.'

'No, she worked hard. Melissa didn't like her though. Not sure about Brendan, but I don't think Brendan really likes any of us.'

'You could be right there!' said Sam. 'What was the problem with Melissa?'

'I don't know. I wasn't in the meetings. All I know is that Anoushka—that was her name—had some tricky phone calls with Melissa. And Melissa sent her some awful emails. Anoushka didn't tell me what was in them, but she did say Melissa was really difficult.'

'I'll probably get the same treatment!'

'Hope not! Anyway, do you want to take this back to your desk, or shall I just show you where it's kept in case you want to look at it again?'

'Let's put it back. I've seen all I need.'

The phone started ringing, and Sam picked it up, listened briefly, and said 'OK, thanks.'

'That was Debbie. Apparently, the police want to see us all in the Board Room at 4:30. I have to say, I didn't think they'd want to get involved with this. I know it looked nasty, but it's really just a bit of unpleasant vandalism.'

'Yeah, true,' said Jen. Her face crumpled again. 'What a way to end the day though.'

Once again, Sam found herself seated at a table looking round at the faces of her colleagues. It was the first time she had seen everyone who worked for Little Bear together. Some looked nervous, and one or two looked annoyed. Brendan looked as though he might explode at any minute. Everyone avoided making eye contact, especially with Brendan.

They didn't have long to wait until two police officers entered the Boardroom, taking the remaining seats. Sam looked up and started slightly.

'Good afternoon, everyone. Thank you for arriving promptly. We'll try not to keep you for long. For those of you I haven't yet spoken to, my name is Detective Sergeant Krystof Balinski, and this is Detective Constable Meera Chaudhury.

'As you know, the company's logo was defaced with a red cross, and a knife was thrust into the logo, penetrating the wall. There was a piece of paper between the wall and the knife point. The paper has a drawing and a message on it. It's not clear who the message was intended for. We will be testing the knife and paper, of course. We believe the perpetrator used nail varnish to paint the cross, and a search of the premises is now underway to see if the bottle is still on site.' Balinski paused as he scanned the faces around the table, gauging the responses to this information.

'We have talked to a number of people already,' he continued, 'prioritising those the receptionist believes had not already left the premises by the time she went home. We will be speaking to all of you separately, and I would remind you, if you have already been interviewed, that you are not to share any of the information you've given me with your colleagues, or anyone outside of the company. We plan to complete interviews by the end of tomorrow.'

'You may be wondering why the police are taking such a close interest in this incident,' Balinski continued. 'I have to inform you that this is not the first time an incident has been reported. There appears to be some kind of vendetta against someone who is working here. Today's incident is a particularly aggressive one, deliberately staged for everyone to see. We will be following a number of lines of enquiry. I have a list of the people we will see tomorrow, and the approximate times you'll need to be available. I'll leave this with Mr McManners.'

Brendan reached reluctantly across the table and took the piece of paper.

'Any questions?' asked DS Balinski, looking around the table. As his eyes met Sam's he blinked in surprise, but he didn't say anything.

'No questions? OK, we'll continue tomorrow,' and left the room with DC Chaudhury following.

'I cannot believe anyone would do this,' hissed Brendan, looking around the table with an expression of fury and dislike. 'If it was any of you, consider yourself sacked—and I'll see you in court. I trust you'll be put away for a long, long time.' The chair he'd pushed back tipped over with a crash, making everyone jump. Ignoring them, Brendan marched out of the office leaving the paper with the list of names and times.

The people left sitting at the table were visibly shocked. Sam heard voices asking 'did you know anything about this?' and 'what incidents?' Nobody had any answers.

One by one people left the room, checking the list as they went out. As Sam walked along the corridor to return to her desk, she heard the phone ring in Brendan's outer office.

Enid, Brendan's timid secretary, answered. Sounding

increasingly nervous, Sam heard her say 'Oh, yes, hello Melissa. No, yes, it has, yes, very unpleasant, yes, I know … I'll put you through.'

Love to be a fly on that wall!' said Sam to herself. '*Sounds as though Melissa's heard something's up. Wonder who told her?*

Back at her desk, it wasn't long before Jen appeared.

'What am I going to do?' she asked Sam. 'I'm being interviewed at 9:30.'

'I'm at 10.'

'What do I say?'

Sam thought for a moment. Should she give advice? Jen was so upset it seemed unkind not to try to help. Sam took a deep breath, and said firmly 'you should tell them some of your drawings have gone missing, just in case there's a connection.' Jen looked alarmed. Sam hurriedly added 'But we don't know that there is.'

'But they'll think it was me,' wailed Jen.

'There's nothing to link you with the knife and the nail varnish. Your drawings aren't a crime,' said Sam. 'It's best to be upfront. Then if it was one of yours on the wall, and the police work that out, you don't look as though you were trying to hide anything.'

Jen didn't look too convinced. 'OK … I suppose. I've got a bad feeling about this though.' She sighed. 'I'd best get home. It'll be another long day tomorrow.'

'Hope you can relax a bit,' Sam said. 'Comfort food and some TV for me, I think!'

Jen gave a small smile and headed off to the toilets. In a few minutes she came rushing back.

'Sam, Sam, it just gets worse,' she cried, looking pale.

'Hey, sit down and get your breath back,' said Sam, pulling out a chair.

'The loo wouldn't flush—the cistern wasn't filling up with water, so I took the lid off and I saw a bottle of red nail varnish. And there's a makeup bag on the shelf under the mirror. I don't know what to do!' she wailed.

'What! Really? Bit of a cliché, hiding it in a cistern! And why has it only just caused a problem? Those loos are in use all day.'

'I know, I know. It's going to look even worse for me.'

'Did you touch anything?'

'No .... No, I didn't.

'Good. Let's see if we can catch the police before they leave. Sam dashed down to reception. The two police officers were just about to go.

'Oh, glad I've caught you.'

Sergeant Balinski raised an eyebrow.

'Oh, yes, sorry, unfortunate choice of words! My colleague thinks she's found the nail varnish. And there's ...'

'Don't tell me here,' cut in Balinski. 'Let's go back to the office we've been using for interviews. I know you, don't I? Didn't you used to work at Kidlington?'

Sam followed the officers to a back office. 'Yes, that's right. I recognised your face too. I've just started working here. It's only my second day but it feels a lot longer!'

'I'm sure. OK, here we are. Come in and sit down. Now tell me. Sorry, I can't remember your name.'

'It's Sam. Sam Holliday,' she said before explaining what had just happened.

'Constable, go and do the necessary with the nail varnish and the bag. They may be connected, maybe not. Block off that cubicle for now. Sam, could you ask your colleague to come to this office please.'

'I'll wait for you upstairs,' Sam said quietly to Jen. Jen gave her a grateful look.

'OK, so you're Jen Somerville?' asked Balinski.

'I am.'

'Take a seat and tell me what you found. When my colleague gets back, I'm going to record this interview. Just let me set up the equipment.'

Jen waited, knees twitching under the table.

'OK,' said Balinski, as DC Chaudhury returned with the bagged-up nail varnish and make-up bag. 'All ready? Off we go,' and he clicked on the recorder.

Chapter Three

Time passed slowly as Sam sat upstairs, waiting for Jen to return for her coat. She sat quietly, turning over the events of the day in her mind. There was little around her to distract her. The windows were night-time dark, and the few posters on the wall were faded and shabby. Her phone bleeped. A text from her mother. That would have to wait. She'd have to think carefully how she summed up day three at Little Bear.

Slow footsteps came up the stairs, and Jen appeared in the doorway.

'OK?' Sam asked, taking in Jen's pale face.

'I think so,' said Jen slowly. 'Hard to tell really. They asked me if I recognised the makeup bag or the nail varnish.'

'And did you?'

'Maybe, I'm not sure …' Jen took a deep breath. 'I think it might be Melissa's.'

'What?'

'Yeah, I know,' said Jen miserably.

'Right, how about you come back to my place. I can throw something together to eat, or we can send out for something. No,' Sam said as Jen started to protest. 'Tonight, we need some good old comfort food, and a nice glass of wine. And some company. What do you say?'

Jen managed a small smile of agreement. 'Thanks, that sounds great. Not sure I'm that hungry, but I'll do my best.'

Krystof Balinski pulled off his jacket and slung it on the back of his chair. Trying to get information out of nervous individuals who either talked too much or said too little always took it out of him. He pushed his fingers through his thick, blond hair which had a habit of falling back into exactly the same place. He rarely looked ruffled, but when he took off his glasses his eyes showed how tired he was. 'Ouf,' he sighed.

'Long day, wasn't it guv?' Meera Chaudhury, the Detective Constable who worked with him, offered sympathetically. Looking up at her, Balinski noticed the tiredness in her face, although her voice sounded bright.

'Yeah. What did you make of them?' he asked.

Meera thought for a moment. 'McManners is going to give himself a heart attack if he carries on getting so angry about everything. And his staff are terrified of him. Well, most of them are. I'm not surprised someone's out to get him. He's a bully.'

'You think all the notes are directed at him? Yeah, I thought that too. Talk me through that. Oh, hey Jack,' he called, spotting a colleague across the office. 'Saw your partner today!'

Jack turned, scowling. 'What partner?'

'Your girlfriend?'

'Huh, ex-girlfriend. We split up.'

'Sorry, I didn't know that.'

'Where did you see her?' asked Jack.

'We had a call out to a publishing company in Lower Rushford. There's a bit of a vendetta going on, and this latest one is a bit vicious.'

'Oh, right. Sam's not involved, is she?'

'Well, she works there, so I'll be interviewing her, along with everyone else.'

'Yeah, 'course,' said Jack. His face registered surprise, and then something more gleeful. 'Cheers, mate. See you around.'

'Yeah, sure.' *What did he mean, 'cheers'?* Krystof wondered briefly as he returned to his conversation with Meera Chaudhury.

'Have you got copies of all the interviews so far? I want to look through them, and see what sense I can make of it all,' he said.

Jen sat with her legs curled underneath her, holding a glass of crisp, dry white wine. 'Delicious wine. Thanks so much for suggesting this. I was dreading going back to my place.'

'Do you live on your own?'

'Yeah, the house is converted into two flats. There are people around, but once I close my front door, it's just me,' said Jen.

Chapter Three

'I didn't want my own company this evening either. Should only be a few minutes until the pizza arrives.'

'When did you move in?' asked Jen.

'A few weeks ago. I didn't bring much stuff with me so that made it easier to get sorted. Oh, there's the bell. That'll be the pizza.'

Returning with two boxes, Sam quickly cut the pizzas into slices and got some plates. 'Dig in before it gets cold!'

'Mmm, smells great. I feel hungry now. I really didn't think I'd eat anything!' said Jen.

'Want to talk about it, or shall we talk about something else?' asked Sam.

'There's not much to tell you, really. I told them about my drawings. They were really interested in that. They showed me the one from today but I'm not allowed to talk about it. And I said I thought the makeup bag was Melissa's, and that she often wears red nail polish. Felt like telling tales.'

'It doesn't mean Melissa did it.'

'No, I don't think even Melissa is that vicious,' said Jen.

'Well ....,' started Sam before catching Jen's eye and laughing. 'No, probably not,' said Sam.

Chapter Four

Thursday, January 20th

An unnatural silence enveloped Sam as soon as she entered Little Bear from the revolving door with her small suitcase and backpack for her train journey later that day. She was hoping she'd still be able to go to Cumbria, but there was a chance Brendan would change his mind, or the police would say everyone had to be on hand for further interviews.

Looking through her notes, she remembered her promise to Stacey Barber, the Production Manager, to follow up on the invoice for the printing of the new *Granny Fi* book.

Why not now? thought Sam, and headed up the stairs to find Clive's office.

His office was on the same floor as Brendan's, although Brendan was not yet in. Nor, it seemed was Clive. Sam knocked again, and then put her head around the door. Empty—and a lot tidier than Brendan and Tony's offices. She decided to go in and write a note for him, asking him to call her when he was free.

Standing at his desk, she had to rummage through a few papers to find something to write on. One piece caught her eye. It was headed 'Golden Lion' with some Chinese lettering alongside. Without thinking about what she was doing, Sam nudged a few other papers to one side so she could read it. It was an invoice from a printer in China—for printing *Granny Fi and the Poorly Bee*. The books *had* been printed. But it wasn't clear if the invoice had been paid.

Heading back down the corridor she almost bumped into Brendan.

'You! What are you doing up here?'

'Good morning, Brendan,' said Sam, hoping she didn't sound as though she'd been caught snooping. 'I was just leaving a message for Clive. I hoped to meet with him this morning.'

'I thought you were going to meet Kaye,' said Brendan, still sounding suspicious.

'I am. I'm leaving this afternoon, if that's still OK.'

'Fine with me. Try not to let on about the events of yesterday. Otherwise I'll have another damned woman nagging at me.'

Sam raised her eyebrows quizzically. 'Oh?'

'You may well say 'oh'. Melissa's breathing down my neck. So you'd better come up with that marketing plan for next week. Don't think I've forgotten.'

'Neither have I. By the way, do you have the last plan—the one Anoushka worked on?'

Brendan gave her a sharp look, presumably surprised she knew her predecessor's name. 'It'll be in my office. Wait in here,' indicating Sam should wait in the outer office. Sam heard him opening a filing cabinet drawer, and shuffling through papers.

While she waited, she glanced idly at Enid's desk. In a basket was a handwritten letter, presumably waiting to be typed. It was partly covering an illustration. A *Granny Fi* illustration, but not in the style Sam was familiar with. Granny Fi's features were different. Her clothes were different. Sam realised that this is how Granny Fi might look if she was drawn for the Chinese market. Odd. She'd have to ask Clive about sales to China.

'Right, here you are. Don't think you can get away with copying it. I wasn't impressed with it. Or with her—whatever her name was.'

'Anoushka?'

'Yes, Anoushka. She didn't last long here,' said Brendan.

'I heard she left suddenly,' said Sam.

'You do when you're fired,' said Brendan, smirking at Sam's shocked expression.

Sam made a coffee and headed back to her desk, just as a call came in.

'You've been in my office,' Clive complained as soon as she answered.

'Yes, I looked in on the off chance that you were in. When I realised you weren't there, I left the note on your desk.'

'Don't do that again,' said Clive.

'OK ...'

'Why do you want to see me?'

'I wanted to ask you if I could have access to the *Granny Fi* sales. Brendan's asked for a marketing plan by the end of next week, and I'm doing some research. I need to see the sales in more detail than I've got at the moment,' Sam explained.

'The system's down today. The IT people are looking in to it. I'll be talking to them, so I'll ask them to set up access for you. I'll let you know when that happens.'

'Oh, thanks, but that's a shame. I'd hoped to look at the figures before I met with Kaye,' said Sam.

'Kaye? She never leaves Cumbria.'

'I'm going to Cumbria to meet her. I want the back story on *Granny Fi*—how the characters were developed, how the illustrations have evolved—that sort of thing.'

'I see.'

'Oh, just one other thing. There seems to be a bit of a mystery around the latest *Granny Fi* book,' Sam said.

'What do you mean?' Clive's tone sharpened.

'Production can't locate the stock. Have we paid the printer, do you know?'

'I'm the Finance Director, not the book-keeper. No, I don't know. There's a lot of invoices going through. I wouldn't expect to see them all.'

'This would have been for quite a large amount of money though.'

'If we'd received the invoice, we would have paid it. Stock is taking a while to get to the warehouse, you know. The pandemic might be over here but it's still causing chaos in China.'

'I realise that.'

'Are we finished now? I've got rather a lot to do this morning.'

'Same here,' said Sam. 'Thanks for your time.'

Well, somebody got out of bed the wrong side this morning, Sam thought to herself. It was puzzling. Where *were* the books? And had the invoice she'd seen on Clive's desk been paid or not? She messaged Stacey quickly, to update her on the little Clive had told her.

It was still early, but on the off chance she decided to call the bookseller Tony Pearson had suggested. The phone rang a few times before it was answered by a brisk-sounding man. Sam explained who she was, and that she wanted to ask about the *Granny Fi* series.

'Dead in the water, in my opinion,' came the prompt reply.

'Really? But it's done so well for so many years. Until this latest story.'

'We're stocked up with all the other stories and we can't shift them. Not taking any more of them. People just don't want to read *Granny Fi* these days.'

'That's a shame. Is there anything else you can tell me? Did you see the latest book?'

'Proof copies, I think. Can't remember what it was about.'

'The poorly bee.'

'Well, that says it all, really. Who wants to pay money to read about a poorly bee?'

'I still don't understand why the sales have dropped so suddenly.'

'New times. Post-pandemic. People want different things.'

'I suppose so,' said Sam hesitantly. 'Well, thanks for talking to me.'

'Pleasure,' and the line went dead.

Chapter Four

Sam sipped her coffee, thinking. It wasn't looking good for *Granny Fi.* Could she really save her favourite character from oblivion?

Jen appeared at Sam's desk with some early daffodils. 'A thank you for yesterday,' she said with a little smile.

'You didn't need to do that, but thanks. How are you feeling?' Sam asked. Jen had clearly given some thought to her appearance, and while she still looked worried, her smart, if colourful, skirt and top made her look in control. 'You look great, by the way!'

'Thought I'd better make an effort,' said Jen, looking nervous. 'I'd rather wear my favourite dungarees, but even I could see they wouldn't make the best impression!'

Sam grinned at her. 'You'll be fine. Good luck. Chat later? I'm leaving for Cumbria this afternoon.'

'Definitely. Good luck to you too.'

Sam read through the marketing plan Brendan had given her. It looked solid enough to her, given the restrictions with social media. All too soon it was approaching 10 and Sam went downstairs for her meeting with the police. There was no sign of Jen.

Her interview was straightforward, as Debbie had confirmed that she and Sam had left the office at the same time. DC Chaudhury then showed her the piece of paper that had been under the knife. It was the drawing Jen had done at the café just a couple of days ago. Sam gasped. Written across the drawing were the words *I'll get you.*

'You recognise this?' asked DS Balinski.

'Yes. But not with—with that writing on it,' Sam said, pointing at it with a trembling finger.

'Tell me more.'

Sam explained what had happened at Gino's. 'Jen's a caricaturist. There's no malice in her drawings.'

'Recognise these?' DC Chaudhury placed four drawings in front of her, each of Brendan, and each with the same word scrawled across them: *murderer*. 'Are you sure there's no malice?'

'I haven't seen these drawings before, only the one that was on the wall. And it didn't have any writing on it when I first saw it.'

'So, what did Jen do with this latest drawing, after she'd shown it to you in the café?'

'She nearly left it behind, but I saw it on the table and she put it in her pocket. It could have fallen out when she took her coat off, back in the office.'

'Hmm. OK, that's all for now,' said Balinski, dismissing Sam.

'I'm meeting one of our illustrators at her home in Cumbria tomorrow, and I'm booked on the train this afternoon. Am I still OK to go?'

'You're not under arrest. Leave the details of where you'll be, how long for, and a contact number with Mr McManners' secretary, and you can go.'

Sam pulled the door closed behind her and breathed a quiet sigh of relief. She hadn't realised quite how tense she was. She headed up the stairs to Enid's office, but Enid wasn't at her desk. The door to Brendan's office was closed, although she could hear him talking on the phone.

The draft letter and the illustration were still in the basket on Enid's desk. Taking out her phone, Sam quickly photographed the letter and the illustration, before writing a note with her contact details on a post-it and sticking it the screen of Enid's computer. As she did so, she noticed the framed photograph Enid was looking at when Sam arrived a couple of days ago for her meeting with Brendan. It showed a happier-looking Enid, with a group of people, some of whom she recognised from Little Bear. The man standing next to Enid looked familiar: like Brendan, but not. *In for a penny,* she thought, and she photographed the framed photo as well.

Jen was waiting for her when she got back to her desk. 'How did it go?' they asked in unison. 'No, you first,' said Sam.

'OK, well, they asked me about the drawings again. Someone has used five of them now, and written over them. Did the police show them to you?'

'Yes, they did. Bit of a shock. I felt as though your drawings had been defaced. What was written on them was horrible.'

'I know. I'm not sure they believed me when I said I hadn't written anything on them.' Jen sighed. 'Melissa's coming in later to see if she can identify her makeup bag and nail polish.'

'We'll all look forward to that then,' said Sam, trying to make Jen laugh. She was rewarded with a small smile.

'Yeah, should be a laugh—not! What about you? How did you get on?'

'I think I'm out of the picture, because Debbie can confirm I left when she did. I told them about you drawing the picture in the café.'

'Yeah. I've drawn quite a few sketches of Brendan. He's a caricaturist's dream, with that nose and furious look. There's a couple more in the drawer that weren't taken because they were under a few folders.'

'Do the police know that? They might be able to use them.'

'How do you mean?'

'Not sure. But maybe to set some kind of trap?'

'Good thinking. I'll ask them, see what they say. Oh, and Sam, thanks for everything. I'll really miss you when you're away.'

'Hey, take my mobile number. You can always message me if you want a chat, or if there's any further developments. I'll be back later on Sunday, and in the office on Monday.'

'Great, thanks. Hopefully there won't be anything that can't wait!'

Light was already fading as Sam left the office. She was dying to take out her phone and look at the letter and illustration she'd photographed in Enid's office, but now wasn't the time or place. Walking through Lower Rushford's town centre to get to the station,

Sam's mind was distracted by the beauty of the old buildings, and the river Rush living up to its name as it flowed rapidly under the old, stone bridge. It didn't seem possible that anyone in Lower Rushford could be capable of such maliciousness, even against Gordon No Manners.

The train line had been one of the reasons Sam had chosen to move to Lower Rushford. That, and of course her new job. Although she had a car, she liked the idea of taking a train to meet up with friends, or to visit new areas for walking trips. Today's journey was not so pleasurable but she was intrigued to meet the formidable-sounding Kaye Butterworth.

Sam found her seat, stowing her luggage in the rack. She took out her phone and notebook, intending to think through what she wanted to ask Kaye. Surprisingly, her part of the train wasn't busy, and she felt she had enough privacy to look at the photo she'd taken of the letter. She read it several times, but she still struggled to make sense of it. It was handwritten, and read:

> *Dear Mr Cheung*
>
> *It was my pleasure to meet with you and your colleagues recently. I trust you found our meeting of interest, and that your time here in the UK was productive for you and your company. I was most impressed with the information you shared with me, and the potential for sales of Granny Fi, if we are able to adapt the stories appropriately for your readership.*
>
> *As discussed, I am sending sample artwork for a new series of Granny Fi stories for you to publish exclusively for your market. The illustrator we are proposing has many years of experience in adapting artwork for other cultures. I trust their work will meet with your approval.*
>
> *I await your response at your convenience, and look forward to discussing further how our organisations can work more closely together, with a view to formalising our partnership in a timely manner.*
>
> *Yours most sincerely*
> *Brendan McManners*
> *Publishing Director, Little Bear Ltd*

There was an email address to send it to. Was Brendan too

important, or too lazy, to send his own emails? Or perhaps he simply didn't 'do' anything digital?

Sam swiped to the second photo. She recognised it immediately as an illustration from a *Granny Fi* story she had read many times to her friend's daughter: *All at Sea with Granny Fi*. But Granny Fi no longer looked like an eccentric and kindly English grandmother. She looked like a rather strict *Chinese* grandmother. Granny Fi's boat looked different and the birds had been re-drawn. The shoreline looked more as she would imagine the coast of China. She swiped between the two photos she had taken, the illustration, and the email text. Why hadn't Brendan sent it himself? And why was he sending it at all? What was going on?

Her brain was whirling with questions—too much for her to focus on her upcoming meeting with Kaye. Eventually the rhythmic movement of the train lulled her into a fitful doze, and she woke with a start with the announcement that the train was approaching the station where she needed to change trains.

The last leg of her journey passed quickly, despite the darkness blocking out any scenery. Arriving in Penrith she picked up her luggage, and went out of the station to find the taxi she'd booked. It felt a lifetime ago that she had done so.

'Evening, miss. Taxi for Holliday? On holiday, are you?' asked the taxi driver, looking pleased with his witticism.

'Oh, that's a new one,' said Sam as brightly as she could manage. 'Yes, I'm Sam Holliday.'

'You're off to the Braithwaite Arms then,' the driver said.

'Just for a couple of nights.'

'Off walking?'

'Hopefully.' Sam didn't want to encourage further conversation. Her head was full of tomorrow's meeting, and the mystery of the email and illustration.

'They do a grand pint, and a good meal by all accounts,' the driver tried again.

'Great, can't wait.'

It seemed a long journey in the darkness along winding, narrow, and hilly roads. The driver took the hint and gave up on any attempts at conversation. Instead, he whistled tunelessly as he followed the contours of the road. The journey seemed never-ending, but eventually some lights came into view: the Braithwaite Arms at last.

Despite the lights in the front windows, it was quiet. No drunken revellers to worry about. Pushing open the heavy wooden door, Sam found herself greeted by the beery fumes and warmth of a bar. Heads turned to see who the newcomer was, and she offered a polite 'good evening'. There were a few acknowledging grunts before heads returned to looking into pint glasses. Sam abandoned her case and backpack at a small table and went up to the bar.

'Hello, love, you must be the lady that's staying with us for a couple of nights?' asked a woman who appeared from a back room. Her plump face, framed by wisps of white hair that had escaped her ponytail, fell naturally into a welcoming smile, and Sam immediately warmed to her.

'Yes, that's me—Sam Holliday. Am I in time to order a meal?'

'You are that. Shall I show you your room, and then you can come down when you're ready and I'll take your order. Kitchen's open for a while longer.'

'Great, thanks.' Sam picked up her luggage and followed the woman through the bar area and up some stairs. Photos of the fells in various weathers adorned the walls, and Sam hoped she'd have time to explore the area a bit before she had to travel home.

'You'll have a lovely view in the morning,' the woman said, slightly breathless from the steep stairs. She paused on the landing and unlocked a door. 'This is you. Not a lot to see outside now,' she said as she swished the curtains closed. The room was small but comfortably furnished. Old-fashioned floral paper matched the bedding. Sam noted the generous number of pillows and cushions, an enormous armchair that could swallow her whole, a small wardrobe, and table with a kettle, mugs, and everything necessary for making hot drinks.

'Your bathroom's through there,' the woman said, pointing to another door.

'It's perfect. I'll be very comfortable here, thank you.'

Chapter Four

'I'm Sandra, by the way. Just shout if there's anything you need. I've put towels out in the bathroom for you. I'll put your key on this table.'

Sam freshened herself up: a brush through her curly hair, and a quick wash of her face and hands and she was ready to return to the bar. *I'm starving* she thought, as she retraced her steps.

She ordered, and sat with her pint of Wainwright, waiting for her homemade pie to appear. She didn't have long to wait, and looking appreciatively at the generous portion, she quickly tucked in, savouring the smell of steak and ale, and the fluffiness of the pastry. Together with a colourful medley of vegetables, it all looked and smelled delicious.

The bar was quiet with, Sam assumed, just a few locals drinking pints. She was surprised the kitchen was open but perhaps there were other guests staying. No one tried to talk to her, and once she'd finished her meal, she was ready to try out the comfortable-looking bed.

Chapter Five

Friday, January 21st

Sam woke to the sound of clattering in the room below her: it must be the kitchen. She reached for her phone. It was already seven o'clock! She'd slept soundly, despite all the questions in her mind, and now her brain was once again buzzing. Her notebook was on the bedside table. She decided to make a cup of tea before returning to bed to jot down the questions she wanted to ask Kaye later that day. Fifteen minutes later she had a good list, and a clearer mind.

Showered and wearing her walking trousers and fleece, Sam made her way down for breakfast, feeling hungrier as the smell of bacon reached her.

'Hello, love, come and sit yourself down in here,' called Sandra. 'Sleep well?'

'Like a log. That bed is really comfortable.'

'Ah, I'm glad to hear it. Now then, what will it be. Full English? Tea, coffee?'

'Coffee, please. And just the bacon and eggs, please. Oh, and a tomato if you have one.'

Sam settled down to wait for her breakfast, happy to admire the view from the windows. For a January day in Cumbria, it was looking rather promising with hints of blue sky, and no rain.

'Here you go,' said Sandra, putting a coffee pot and some toast on the table. 'This'll keep you going while I finish your bacon and eggs.'

'Thanks. Looks like a nice morning.'

'Yes. If you wanted a walk, there's a good path that goes up behind the pub. It takes you to a small tarn you can walk round. It's a lovely walk, and you can't really get lost.'

'Sounds perfect. I might give it a go.'

Sandra soon reappeared with Sam's breakfast. The bacon didn't look anything like the rashers she bought at the supermarket, and the egg yolks glowed a golden yellowy-orange. It all tasted every bit as good as it looked.

Sam collected her walking boots and backpack from her room. Sandra was clearing the breakfast things, and Sam called out that she was going on the walk Sandra had suggested.

'Oh, I'm visiting Kaye Butterworth at Hawksmoor Cottage later today. Is it far from here?' Sam asked.

'Kaye's place? No, not far. Just head down the hill and take the first left. You can't miss it. Relative, are you?'

'No, I'm meeting her about her illustrations.'

'Ah, she's a grand artist. Keeps herself to herself though.'

'So I've heard. I'm really pleased she's agreed to meet me,' said Sam as she laced her boots and hoisted her backpack onto her back. It was bigger than she needed for her walk today, but she'd put her waterproof trousers in, and some water.

Outside, she stood for a moment and looked around at the cluster of grey-stone houses with their backdrop of moorland and rising fells. There was a brisk breeze which pushed the clouds along, casting shadows as they passed by, changing the greens of the moorland grass from light to dark. Breathing in the sharp, fresh air, she realised how she'd missed the outdoors after a short spell in the office. Turning to face the pub, she saw the path snaking upwards, over the fell and into the distance. It would be a good, steep climb to work off her breakfast.

Twenty minutes later she was feeling considerably warmer, and was still climbing. She stopped to catch her breath and to admire the view. The small settlement and its surrounding moors were spread out below her, looking as idyllic as a model village. Her heart rate settled, and she carried on along the rough stones of the footpath. After following the path for a few more twists and turns, the promised tarn suddenly appeared. Winter sunlight shimmered on the water's silvery surface, which was ruffled by the breeze. She had the place to herself. A flat rock invited her to rest a while, and she sat, quietly appreciating the sound of the breeze through the grasses.

The quietness was broken by a sharp buzz from her phone. She sighed, and taking it out of her backpack, checked for messages. Two texts, one from her mother and one from Jen. Her mother could wait. Jen would only text if it was urgent.

Melissa's going ballistic! Sam read. '*It's her nail varnish—and her makeup bag!!! She's demanding we're all arrested or she'll never write another book for us again!!!!*' Sam couldn't help smiling at the number of exclamation marks. It wasn't difficult to imagine the drama Melissa would make of the situation.

She'll get over it. The police haven't got enough cells for everyone, Sam replied, and she added a smiley emoji that she hoped would cheer Jen up. She hit send, and her phone promptly pinged again.

Can't wait for u to get back here Jen replied. Sam gave a quick 'thumbs up' in reply.

Sam quickly replied to her mother, and checked the time. It looked quite a short walk around the tarn so she decided to continue. Following the path, she admired the tarn's clean-looking water, and the backdrop of the fells unfolding into the distance. Eventually she returned to her starting point, ready to head downhill to the pub. As she started to walk down, her foot slipped on a loose stone, and she yelped as she turned her ankle over. Feeling queasy with the sudden pain, she sat down and put her fingers down the side of her boot to see if she could feel any damage. It seemed OK. She wiggled her foot. That didn't hurt. She tried to stand, but as soon as she put her weight on the ankle the stabbing pain made her gasp out loud.

No! she thought, *what do I do now?*

The quietness of the morning which she'd found so tranquil just minutes ago suddenly took on a more sinister feel as she faced her options. She could only think of two: stay where she was in the hope Sandra would raise the alarm, or try to limp her way down. She decided to try limping. It wasn't that far to the pub, and she would get cold if she sat where she was for long.

Progress was agonisingly slow. Biting her lip, every step required all her willpower to insist her ankle took her weight. Her steps were ungainly, but looking back over her shoulder she could see she had made some progress. Concentrating on not missing her footing again, she almost cannoned into a walker coming up the hill.

'Oops, sorry, I thought you'd seen me,' said a bright, cheery voice. 'Is everything all right? You look as though you're limping.' The voice had a note of concern in it now, and looking at him Sam saw a hint of a frown above blue eyes and a beard.

'Limping? Of course I'm limping. I've sprained my ankle,' Sam snapped.

'Oh no, can I help at all?' asked the walker.

'If you could make this path about a mile shorter, that would be a start.'

'Um, I was thinking more along the lines of lending you my walking poles?' The man smiled wryly at her.

'Oh, thanks, yes. Sorry. They probably would help,' said Sam, looking at the poles and avoiding looking at the man, who had been more gracious than she'd deserved.

'Where do you have to get back to?' he asked.

'Just to the pub. It's not far, but walking on this ankle is so painful!'

'I know. It's happened to me before. Look, why don't I walk back with you, just to make sure you're OK? I mean, I'm sure you'll be fine, but …'

'No, you're right. It would be better to go together. Thank you.'

'Here you go,' he said, handing over the poles. 'I'll leave you to adjust them to the length you want.'

'Thanks.' There was a pause while Sam fiddled with lengthening the poles for the downhill walk. 'OK, let's try this.'

The way down didn't feel quite so intimidating now she had company, and the two poles took some of the weight off her injured ankle. Leading the way, the man warned her where the stones were particularly loose, or where she needed to take extra care, but didn't try to make conversation. Sam concentrated on keeping herself moving. It was annoying not to be able to go at her usual speed, but even so the pub soon came into sight.

'I've never been so glad to see a pub!' said Sam.

'I bet! I'm Nate, by the way. I live in one of the cottages just along the road.'

'Oh, so you have all this walking on your doorstep! Lucky you! I'm Sam. I'm just here for a couple of days to meet with Kaye Butterworth. I've got to get to her cottage this afternoon.'

'Why don't you hang on to the poles then. Kaye doesn't live far from the pub, but your ankle's not going to get better by this afternoon, unfortunately.'

'That's kind of you. Hey, if you're in the pub this evening I'll buy you a drink as a thank you,' Sam offered.

'Well, I won't say no to that,' Nate grinned. 'I usually look in around 8. Does that work for you?'

'Perfect. Now I'd better get myself sorted for this afternoon. See you later—and thanks.' Nate smiled. Sam turned away to open the door to the pub and to face the steep stairs to her room.

Fumbling with the walking poles, and trying to work out the best way to get upstairs, she ended up dropping the poles with a clatter that alerted Sandra.

'Hello? Oh, it's you, Sam. Good walk?'

'It was beautiful, but I turned my ankle on the way down. Someone called Nate was walking up—luckily—and he lent me his walking poles.'

'Oh dear, what bad luck. Good thing Nate was around. He's a

local lad. Knows these fells like a Herdwick sheep! What about an ice pack for that ankle? Can you manage the stairs?' Sam hobbled to the first step and looked up, not sure how to answer Sandra.

'Let's get you in here and have a look at it,' said Sandra, indicating a small room off the bar area. 'Sit yourself down and I'll get some ice.'

'Ouf,' was all Sam could say as she eased herself into a saggy-looking chair. She untied her boot laces, and gently eased off her boot. The ankle immediately started to swell, and there was already some bruising. An ice pack was definitely needed.

'Here, put your foot up on this,' Sandra said, moving a stool in front of Sam's armchair. 'Let's have a look. Oh, it doesn't look too bad. Can you move your ankle?'

Sam tried, rather gingerly. The ankle did move, but it was painful. 'I don't think I've broken anything. I couldn't have got down the hill if I had,' she said.

'True. Right then, keep the ice on for ten minutes or so, and I'll be back.'

'I've got to get to Kaye's for two. Nate's loaned me his poles so I can use them to walk down.'

'I can drive you there, if needs be,' Sandra offered.

'You're very kind, but let's see how it is after I've used the ice.'

'OK. How about some painkillers, and a cup of tea? You've had a bit of a shock.'

Sam nodded gratefully to both offers. She sat back in the armchair and closed her eyes. Sandra was right. Turning her ankle had shaken her. What a nightmare it all was! Now she'd have to turn up at Kaye's limping, and she would have to own up to a stupid accident. It wasn't quite the image she wanted to present. She shook her head. This wouldn't do. She'd get to Kaye's, have the meeting, and get back to the pub. Everything else—the photos, the drawings, Brendan's threat of firing her—would all have to wait.

Chapter Five

An hour later, she felt rested and ready to face getting changed for her meeting. There was no chance of wearing the smart ankle boots that went so well with her trousers: her foot was too swollen.

Sam made her way carefully down the stairs and out of the pub onto the lane. Checking the names on the cottages as she went—none of them had numbers—she realised that Kaye's was the furthest away—of course. Arriving at the front door of Hawksmoor Cottage, she lifted the impressive black knocker and tapped a rat-a-tat-tat. There was an immediate bark in response.

Sam heard Kaye reassuring the dog, sounding gentler than she had on the phone. *Note to self, make friends with the dog,* Sam thought as she waited for the door to be opened.

'Yes?'

It wasn't the most welcoming of greetings but the voice was sterner than the face. Silvery-grey hair, cut in a no-nonsense bob framed a long face that looked younger than Sam had expected. Clear grey eyes looked enquiringly at Sam, who hastily introduced herself.

'You're on time, at least. Come in, we're letting the cold in, standing here.' Kaye looped her fingers through the dog's collar and held him to one side so Sam could pass. The fingers were slightly stained with paint. 'This is Gustav. You needn't be nervous of him. He doesn't bite.'

'Hey, Gustav,' Sam said as she fondled Gustav's head. His tail beat against Kaye's trouser legs, which also had traces of paint.

'Thanks for making time to see me. I appreciate you're busy.'

There was a dismissive snort as Kaye led the way to the sitting room. 'Sit down. We can talk here. Tea?'

'Please. Can I do anything?'

'Yes, stay there and talk to Gustav. We don't get many visitors.'

For once, Sam was happy to do as she was told. Gustav was a golden brown lurcher with long bendy legs, and a narrow head with a long nose that he pushed into Sam's lap. Two intelligent eyes looked her over carefully. Clearly he agreed with Kaye. They didn't get many visitors so he for one was going to make the most of Sam's company. His tail thumped against the floor as she patted him.

It was a comfortable room, with a small sofa and chairs arranged around the glowing wood-burning stove, and shelves of books in the alcoves. The stove gave out some welcome warmth. At the window, a wide seat built into the wall of the cottage gave a good view of the lane, and over the moorland to the rising fells. Even on a cold January day it looked beautiful.

Kaye returned with a tray of tea and cakes. 'I see you've made a friend of Gustav.'

'He's gorgeous. Is he Gustav for Holst or Mahler?

'Holst, of course.'

Sam wasn't sure why it should be so obvious, but as she'd already stretched her musical knowledge to the limit, she decided not to comment further. 'Of course,' she murmured.

'Well then, what do you want to talk to me about?'

Sam reached for her notebook, and glanced down at her list of questions. 'Perhaps we could start with how Little Bear came about, and how you became the illustrator for the *Granny Fi* stories.'

'Good grief, how long are you planning on staying? That was years ago!' Kaye glanced at Sam and saw her questions were serious. 'If you're sure you want all that history, then we'd better get started. Pour the tea!'

Sam did as she was asked, and handed a cup to Kaye. The walking poles clattered to the floor.

'What on earth do you need those walking poles for? It's only a few yards from the pub, and it's along a tarmac road!' asked Kaye as Sam propped the poles up again.

'I went for a walk this morning, and turned my ankle. Someone called Nate was on the same footpath, and kindly lent me his poles. They help.'

'Oh, Nate.' Kaye's voice softened. 'He lives a few doors along. Nice man. A keen walker, and a good writer. Keeps himself to himself.'

'Sounds the ideal neighbour,' Sam sipped her tea, and decided it was best to make a start. 'I really would like to hear how you and your sister came to set up a publishing company.'

Kaye sighed. 'It was in the early 1980s. I'd finished at art school and was trying to make a career as an illustrator. My sister, Charlotte, was already working for a publisher in London. Our father had recently died and left us some money, and we thought we'd try to set up our own business. Charlotte was married, and wanted to start a family. I think she thought that running a business would give her more flexibility. I suppose it did in a way, but those first few years were hard.' Kaye paused, a faraway gaze in her eyes. 'Are you sure you want to hear all this?'

'Yes, I really do! How did you build it up? And when did Granny Fi appear?'

'Granny Fi didn't happen for some time. We gradually got a few authors on our books, and some agents started sending book proposals our way. We had a few modest successes, and then Melissa appeared with these adventure stories with an eccentric Granny. The stories needed an illustrator. Charlotte showed the stories to me to see if I'd be interested, and I was. The first book was *Granny Fi scoots to tea*. Everyone: Charlotte, Melissa, the sales people, thought my illustrations worked so we went ahead and published the book. The rest you probably know. Initially, we brought out two books a year, one for Christmas and the other for summer. Always hardback in those days. And they sold, in surprisingly big numbers, so we brought out more. It was the making of Little Bear. We've never had a series like it.'

'And now?' prompted Sam

'Well, I hear the sales have plummeted. I suppose it had to happen one day.'

'Why do you think it's happened now?'

Kaye looked uncomfortable. 'I think—well, it doesn't matter what I think. We've just reached the end of our run,' and she stood up with the tray and walked briskly to the kitchen.

When she returned, Sam asked 'Everyone knows Granny Fi. She's so distinctive. How did she come about? Did you immediately see her that way?'

'Yes, I did. I've got some of my early drawings in my studio room. Can you manage with your poles? It would be best to look at them there.'

'Yes, it's probably time to move. Sorry, I'll take a minute or two to get going. It's painful when I first put my weight on it.'

'Gustav, come here. She doesn't need you tripping her up,' and Kaye took a firm hold of Gustav's collar. Gustav looked up at Sam, tongue slightly out, as though he was having a quiet laugh about the folly of walking on two legs.

Sam followed Kaye into a small room filled with wintry light. With larger windows than the sitting room it was ideal for drawing, although it was a much colder room. Sam shivered slightly, and snuggled in to her fleece.

'I did warn you it was cold here. We won't stay long.' Kaye opened a drawer and took out a large, bulky folder. 'Here we are. These are my first sketches. You can see how Granny Fi evolved. Quite quickly, really.'

'These are lovely,' said Sam looking at the drawings laid out on the table. The colours were still vibrant, and Granny Fi's eccentric personality shone through. 'Is she fun to draw?'

'She is. Until she met a poorly bee. I hate drawing bees. I can never get the wings right.'

'So why did Melissa write a story with a bee in it?'

Kaye sighed, and Sam waited for her to speak. 'Melissa and I are very different, and it's surprising really that our working relationship has lasted this long. Frankly, I think she's reached the end of the road with Granny Fi, and wants a way out.'

'Interesting. She didn't give me that impression when I met her earlier this week. She was furious about the sales, and even more angry when Brendan suggested Granny Fi had had her day.'

'Well, she wouldn't want to admit she's had enough. That's not her style. All that ranting is just a smoke screen to save her dignity,' said Kaye, looking scornful. 'Right, I'll put these away and we can go back into the warm.'

Sam hobbled after Gustav, and sat back into the sofa. Outside, the afternoon light was fading fast. Kaye drew the curtains, blocking out the dusk.

'What else can I tell you?'

Chapter Five

'Could you talk me through how you went about drawing one of the illustrations for one of the stories. Perhaps you have a favourite?'

'I do. All right, let me find it.' Kaye went to the bookshelves and pulled out a book. Here we are. '*Granny Fi has fun at the fair*. Fun to draw, too.' Kaye settled back into her armchair and started to talk, while Sam listened, taking occasional notes.

'Have you ever thought about selling the rights to *Granny Fi*, for publishing in another country?' Sam asked as Kaye finished talking.

'It has come up from time to time, but we've preferred to keep the rights with Little Bear. Granny Fi is such an English granny, you'd have to make a lot of changes for her to appeal to children elsewhere.'

'What about China? Learning English is really taking off there, and that would be a really big market.'

'Humph. Brendan was talking about that at the last Board meeting. I said over my dead body. Granny Fi is Granny Fi. I'm not re-inventing her as a granny for Chinese children. I'm sure they have more than enough stories of their own. If Brendan wants to do that, he'll have to get rid of me first.'

'I can see why you feel that way,' said Sam, feeling sympathetic to Kaye. 'Anyway, I'm going to start working on the marketing when I get back to the office. Is there anything you think we should be doing to help sales?'

'Getting the books in front of the customer usually works.'

'True. And I gather there's been some problems with that.'

'Really?'

'Yes. The bookseller I spoke to didn't even remember seeing the actual book—just proof copies. The sales manager says bookshops didn't want to take it.'

'Can't say I blame them really.'

'Why's that?'

'It wasn't Melissa's best story by any means. And a weak story, combined with illustrations which were not my best, probably wasn't going to make it a bestseller.'

'The people I've spoken to are assuming it's because times have changed, and Granny Fi has lost her appeal.'

'Possible, of course.' Kaye thought for a moment. 'But I always thought Granny Fi was timeless. That was part of her charm. She was a granny everyone loved, and she had crazy adventures, but you always knew everything would end well.'

'I agree. I used to read them to a friend's daughter and she loved them. Well, we both did. It's one of the reasons I took the job!'

Kaye smiled at her, and the two women sat in companionable silence for a few moments.

'Well, I think we've done all we can for today. If you think of anything else before you travel back, just call. I'm in all day tomorrow. I need to walk Gustav before it gets much darker,' said Kaye.

'It's been really good to hear about the background to the stories, and to Little Bear. Thank you. I'll be in touch if I think of anything else.'

'Surprisingly, I've rather enjoyed this afternoon,' said Kaye with a small smile. 'Will you be all right getting back to the pub?'

'Yes, it's not far, and the poles really do help.'

'Let me open the door for you. Gustav, no, you're not going with her,' and Kaye grabbed Gustav's collar before he could take himself off with Sam.

Kaye closed the door quietly, and released her hold on Gustav's collar.

'Don't get yourself settled,' she warned him. 'It's time for your evening walk.' Gustav's tail thumped the floor enthusiastically. It would take more than a dark, cold evening to deter him.

Changing into her boots, and putting on a warm coat in preparation for a leisurely walk to allow Gustav time to enjoy the many interesting smells he would no doubt find, she thought back over the afternoon. It had been a long time since anyone had taken such a genuine interest in her work. Usually, her drawings were viewed as a means to an end: to sell as many books as possible. She hoped she'd given Sam enough information to help her marketing plans, and that more children would discover the books as a result.

Chapter Five

'Right, Gustav. Let's go. Then we can come home and put our feet up for the rest of the evening,' said Kaye. Gustav looked up, and gave a small 'woof' of agreement.

Sam hobbled slowly out to the lane. The light had now gone, and she was glad it wasn't far. Suddenly, bright headlights appeared further along the lane and a dark-coloured car sped quickly towards her. It seemed unnecessarily fast for the narrow lane, and Sam instinctively stepped back, wincing at the pain caused by the sudden movement. As the car went by, she vaguely noticed it was a Nissan Qashqai. She couldn't really see the driver, but there was something in the way he was hunched over the steering wheel that reminded her of Brendan's pent-up anger. Of course, it couldn't be Brendan. He was in Lower Rushford. *I've got Brendan on the brain,* she muttered to herself, and turned to walk slowly back to the pub.

Sitting at the table in his sitting room, Nate saw the silhouette of a figure with a hobbling walk. It had to be Sam. Watching her, he realised he was holding his breath, anxious she might fall again. She'd been a bit sharp with him at first but he knew now that was more to do with the shock of turning her ankle. She'd seemed a lot nicer once she'd got back to the pub and knew she was safe. He was wary of new people, especially women, but the offer of a drink at the pub later had been friendly rather than flirtatious. He'd probably wander down later. But before that, he wanted to get some writing finished. *Wonder how Kaye got on with Sam*, he thought.

Sam sat on the edge of the bed, thinking. Clearly Kaye had no idea that Brendan had pursued his plans to publish in China. What was he playing at? And what would it take to persuade Kaye that Little

Bear needed to look for sales elsewhere to survive? She certainly understood that sales were declining, but she seemed accepting of that.

Her phone pinged, and she opened a text from Jen. *The trap is set.* Sam knew exactly what that meant: one of Jen's drawings had been left where it could be found. Presumably there was surveillance in place, or perhaps the paper would simply be tested for fingerprints. She wasn't too sure how the police worked.

Interesting times she messaged in reply.

She took out her notebook, and jotted a few ideas that had occurred to her after talking with Kaye: ideas that she could work into her marketing plan. It was hard to concentrate with a throbbing ankle, and with her mind buzzing about the China mystery, let alone everything that was happening at Little Bear. She put the notebook aside, and started getting herself ready to go down to the bar to eat. Would Nate come in for a drink? Did she hope he would? He'd certainly been kind to her, as a fellow walker.

It was quiet in the bar, with just a few men sipping their pints of beer. Sam nodded a good evening, and took a seat at the bar while she waited for someone to serve her.

'Ah, there you are,' said Sandra, appearing from the kitchen, swathed in a large apron. 'How have you got on?'

'I managed the walking OK. And I met Kaye, and Gustav of course. She's such an interesting person. And a very talented artist.'

'She is. Sounds as though she took a shine to you. She isn't known for being chatty.'

'I can imagine. But we were talking about things that are important to her, and I think that made the difference. Gustav seemed to like me, which went down well.'

'It certainly would. She's devoted to that dog. Or should I say he's devoted to her? Anyway, what can I get you this evening?'

Her meal ordered and soon eaten, Sam was thinking about getting a second glass of wine when Nate came in. Unravelling a warm scarf from his neck, he called across to her 'Hi, Sam. How's things?' That made a few heads turn, as the locals nodded at Nate and looked curiously at her.

Chapter Five

'Hi, Nate. What are you drinking?

'Well, if you're sure, I'll have a pint of the special.'

Seated on opposite sides of the small table, Sam wondered how to open the conversation.

'Kaye tells me you're a walker, and a writer,' seemed as good a start as any.

Nate smiled. 'Yes, to both. It would be a bit of a waste to live here and not enjoy the walking—in my opinion, anyway. And walking and writing seem to go together.'

'What sort of thing do you write?'

'Non-fiction. Books for walkers, or armchair walkers, about the landscape, its history, its language.'

'Sounds interesting.'

'Well, I enjoy it. I work with a small publisher, and the books do quite well in the local shops, and on Amazon, of course. People don't have to live here to love this part of the world, and they seem to enjoy reading about it. Which is good news for me! What about you, what do you do?'

Sam explained her recent move to Little Bear, and her love of the *Granny Fi* stories and the connection with Kaye. Nate was a good listener, judging by the questions he asked from time to time. Conversation flowed well, and they moved on to talking about walking, favourite routes, and ideas for future walks they'd each like to do. The time passed quickly, and the bell for last orders took them both by surprise.

'It's been great talking to you, Sam. Look, here's my card if you're this way again and want to meet up for a walk or a drink.'

Sam took the card, amused that he was old-fashioned enough to have one. She now had Nate's contact details, but did she want them? Suddenly she felt unsure. The invitation was very casual, and she had enjoyed spending time with him. She decided to play for time.

'Nate Braithwaite, writer and photographer,' she read. 'Braithwaite. That's the same name as this village.'

'Yes, back in the day our family were landowners here. But the estate's long gone.'

'I see. Well, thanks Nate. I may take you up on that walk sometime. Any chance I could keep the walking poles until I go home tomorrow? I may meet with Kaye again tomorrow morning. I could leave them here, behind the bar, if you don't mind picking them up?'

'That's fine. I usually pop in during the week. Just let Sandra know.'

They both stood up. There was a moment of awkwardness as they both hesitated. Should they shake hands? Hug? After a slight pause Nate picked up his scarf and started to wrap up again for the walk home. 'Bye then,' he said with a small wave as he turned the handle on the old, heavy wooden door to let himself out into the night air.

By the time Sam got into bed, she was feeling pleasantly sleepy. Nate's face came into her mind. An honest face, she thought. Caring, friendly. Not particularly handsome, but a good face. Other faces floated into her mind. Brendan, all fury and bad temper—the opposite to Nate. And a face she vaguely recognised. Like Brendan's, but without the anger. Where had she seen it? She drifted off to sleep.

Chapter Six

Saturday, January 22nd

Sam awoke next morning to the now familiar noise of Sandra in the pub kitchen. Tentatively, she rolled off the side of the bed, and put her feet to the floor. Her ankle was less swollen, but it felt stiff, and protested when she put her weight on it. *Not as bad as yesterday,* she thought, as she eased herself to standing and slowly made her way to the bathroom. *Not sure I'm ready for Helvellyn just yet though.*

A little later she had hobbled her way down the stairs to find Sandra waiting for her. 'Good morning, Sam. Oh, your ankle seems better. That's good. Sleep well?'

'I did, thanks. Yes, it's getting there. Just needs a bit more rest.'

'Go and make yourself comfortable, and I'll bring your breakfast through. Same as yesterday?'

'That would be lovely, thank you.'

A few minutes later Sandra appeared with a pot of coffee and some toast. 'Looked as though you were enjoying your chat with Nate last night,' she commented.

'Oh, yes, I did. He was telling me about his books, and the walks he's done.'

'He's done well for himself since he came out the police force.'

'He didn't mention being a policeman.'

'No, he doesn't talk about it much. Think he's really absorbed in his writing, and the police work is all in the past.'

Sam poured some coffee, and sat, thinking. The mention of the police force was unsettling. She gave a little shake of her head. She was being silly. Not every police officer was like Jack Henshaw. And she only had to see Nate again if she chose to make the effort to do so.

Her thoughts were rudely interrupted by a pounding on the front door.

'What on earth …,' she heard Sandra exclaim. 'All right, I'm on my way,' Sandra called. She opened the door, and Nate stepped in.

'I need to talk to you, Sandra.'

'What's the matter?'

'Let's go in to the bar.'

Sam heard their footsteps, and the door to the bar opening and closing. She turned her attention to her breakfast. *What was going on?*

She'd just finished eating when Sandra and Nate came into the room.

'Sam, love, Nate's got some difficult news to tell you,' Sandra said. Her hands plucked at her apron and she looked worried.

Nate pulled out a chair, and sat at Sam's table.

'What's happened?' Sam asked, puzzled.

'It's Kaye, I'm afraid.'

Sam looked at him, not sure what he was saying. She read concern and sadness in his face. 'What do you mean?'

'I woke up in the early hours and heard howling. When I went out to investigate, I realised it came from Kaye's house. No one answered the door so I broke in. And …' his voice cracked and he cleared his throat before continuing. 'And I found Kaye, on the floor. Sam, I'm afraid Kaye's dead.' He looked up at Sam, but he wasn't seeing her. From the look of horror on his face he was once again looking at Kaye's body.

'Dead? But I only saw her yesterday! Was it … was it a heart attack or something?'

Chapter Six

'No .... No, it wasn't. Sam, there's no easy way to tell you this. It looks as though Kaye was murdered.'

'What?' Sam looked from Nate to Sandra, not wanting to take in the full horror of Nate's news. Two pale faces looked back at her.

'How can that be? I don't believe it!' said Sam.

'The police are there now. It's not confirmed, but from what I saw, that's what I'm expecting them to say. I'm so sorry, Sam. This must be a horrible shock to you,' and he reached out to gently squeeze her arm.

'Yes. Yes, it is. And for you. For both of you,' she said as she started to absorb what Nate had told her. 'I mean, you knew her much better than I did. I just met her for one afternoon.'

'No one knew her very well. She was a private person. But she's lived here a long time, and it will be a shock to everyone here. If she'd died naturally, that would be bad enough. But murder?' Sandra wiped her eyes with a corner of her apron.

'Sorry to ask, but when were you planning to leave? It's just that I expect the police will want to talk to you. You were probably one of the last people to see her alive,' said Nate.

'Oh no ... yes, they will. I've got a train ticket for this afternoon. But I may need to stay on. Sandra, could I book the room for another night if I need to stay?'

Sandra nodded. 'That's no problem, we're not busy this time of the year. Oh dear. I think we all need a cup of tea. I'll get the kettle on,' and she went out to make herself busy.

Nate and Sam sat quietly together at the table. 'I don't suppose you can tell me why you're so sure she was murdered, can you?' Sam asked.

'Best not,' Nate replied.

'It must have been a huge shock. Oh, and what about Gustav? He must be distraught.'

'He's a very unhappy dog. I've got him at my house for now. I'd better get back soon—he'll be anxious. I just wanted to break the news to you before you heard it from the police.'

'Thanks, I appreciate it,' said Sam with a small smile. 'Could I come with you to see Gustav?'

'I'm sure Gustav would love to see you. He's very unsettled. I think he'd appreciate someone else to make a fuss of him. It's not far to my place. I'm at the same end of the village as Kaye. Why don't we have a cup of tea with Sandra, and then we can go.'

Nate automatically walked quickly, anxious to get home to Gustav and out of the northerly wind that blew into their faces. Looking back at Sam, he slowed his pace.

'I'm not usually such a slow coach!' she said, as she finally caught up with him.

'I forgot about your ankle, sorry. It's not really the weather for hanging around, is it?'

'Not really, but this is my top speed at the moment.'

As they walked further along the lane, two parked police cars came into view, with the blue and white tape blocking entry onto Kaye's property. As they got closer, Nate called 'Hi, Dan' to the policeman standing outside Kaye's front door.

'Morning, Nate. So, this is where you hang out,' commented the policeman, eyeing Sam speculatively.

'Yeah, my place is just here,' said Nate, indicating his cottage. 'How's things with you, Dan?'

'All right, considering,' Dan replied, giving a nod to the door behind him.

'You're probably going to want to talk to Sam here. She had a meeting with Kaye yesterday. About work,' he added.

'I'll be at Nate's, or at the pub—that's where I'm staying,' said Sam helpfully.

'I'll tell the gaffer, and we'll let you know,' said Dan.

'Would that be Bob Keld?' asked Nate.

'Yep, it's his case.'

'Not retired yet then,' grinned Nate.

'Retirement? I think it would kill him,' and the two men chuckled quietly.

'Can't imagine the force without him. Right, see you around,

Dan. Now then, let's get out of this cold,' said Nate, taking out his door key There were a couple of barks, followed by some whining, as Nate unlocked the door, and Gustav hurtled out, whether to greet them or to escape back to his old home wasn't clear. Nate grabbed Gustav's collar, and encouraged the dog back inside.

Stepping into the small entrance hall and from there, the sitting room, Sam was reminded of Kaye's cottage although Nate's was presented very differently. Similarly uncluttered, it was nonetheless comfortable with leather armchairs, shelves of books, and a small desk with a laptop and notebook. The pictures were mainly line drawings of wildlife. Nate saw her looking at them and said 'My sister's work. She keeps giving them to me and I have to have them on display.'

'They're really good. She's very talented.'

'I know. No, it's no hardship having them. I just don't have room for anything else! Anyway, make yourself comfortable.'

Sam sat down, and Gustav laid his head on her lap, looking up at her enquiringly, as if waiting for some explanation of recent events. 'Poor old boy,' said Sam, smoothing the top of his head. 'I expect he'll need a walk soon.'

'Yes, probably. If you're OK, I'll just take him out for a few minutes. I don't want him doing a runner back to Kaye's though.'

'Have you got something you can use as a lead? Is he used to a lead?'

'Yes, he is. I'll get a belt and loop it through his collar. If I go the opposite way to Kaye's there's a footpath that leads on to the moor. Should be enough of a walk for him for now.' Nate went to sort out the makeshift lead, and put it on Gustav who looked a little affronted. 'Come on, Gustav, it's for your own good. We don't want to lose you.'

Gustav retorted with a small woof, and followed Nate out of the door. 'Won't be long. Make yourself at home,' called Nate as he went out.

Sam settled back into the chair, trying to relax. Memories of yesterday's meeting with Kaye came into her mind. The beautiful drawings, Kaye's genuine enjoyment of the *Granny Fi* stories and of creating the illustrations over many years. Her insistence that she would never adapt them to sell elsewhere. Sam sat up with a start. The car she'd seen: what if it had been Brendan? What if he had tried to persuade Kaye that they had to publish in China, but with a different illustrator? What if Kaye had refused? *Could* Brendan have killed her? No … no, he might not be a very nice man, but that didn't make him a murderer. But someone thought he was a murderer, because that was the word they had written over Jen's drawings of him.

The figure she'd seen hunched over the steering wheel of the Qashqai came back to her. The profile was very like Brendan's. But any tall, bulky man who was driving a bit aggressively would look the same. The light hadn't been good enough to know for sure.

She thought about Brendan's face, and suddenly she remembered a similar face she'd seen recently. Where had it been? On the train? At work? She couldn't place it. She got her phone out to check for messages. Nothing. Should she delete the photos she took of Brendan's email and the drawings? She opened her photos to look at them again. Did they hold the key to Kaye's murder?

Opening up her photos, she looked again at the one she had taken of the framed photo on Enid's desk. Yes! There was the face she'd been thinking about: the man who was like Brendan. Whoever he was looked on friendly terms with Enid. Suddenly, she realised who she was looking at. It was Frank McManners, Brendan's brother. The one who had had a heart attack and fallen down the stairs. The one Enid had found. Had Frank and Enid been more than colleagues, and was that important? Sam decided she needed to find out more.

She texted Jen. *Have some very sad news. Kaye has died suddenly. Huge shock. Keep it to yourself for now. Sorry to ask, but do you know if Enid and Frank were an item? Hope you're OK.*

Nate hadn't yet returned, so she got up to browse his bookshelves. There was just one photo, of a younger Nate with a woman. She didn't look like Nate so she assumed the woman was a partner. Ex-partner? He hadn't mentioned anyone, and the house felt more like a bachelor pad than a cosy home for two. It was none of her business, she thought, and continued looking along the shelves. More non-fiction than fiction. Even some poetry! If she didn't know already, she would have worked out from his book choices that he had a deep interest in land, nature, walking and climbing. She wondered what the books he wrote were like. They must be good to sell well enough to provide an income.

She picked out a book of Noman MacCaig's poetry and had just started reading when she heard the door open, and the clatter of Gustav's paws on the flagstones.

'Hey, Gustav, nice walk?' she asked. Gustav gave a lukewarm wag of his tail, once again laying his head on her lap so she could stroke him. 'It's all right, Gustav, you're safe here.'

'Hi, Sam. Oh good, you found something to read. What have you got? Ah, Norman MacCaig. He's a favourite of mine. His descriptions always amaze me. Spot on, and in so few words.'

'I'd only just picked it up, but yes, I can see what you mean. How was Gustav?'

'A bit lacklustre, to be honest. He made a token effort at checking out the smells, but he soon wanted to come back indoors. He's not himself, that's for sure,' and he came across to give Gustav a pat. Gustav thumped his tail on the carpet a couple of times in acknowledgement. 'Poor old boy. I'll keep him here for the time being. Otherwise, he's going to be homeless and we can't have that. Kaye will start haunting me!'

'He's lucky you can take him on.'

There was a pause in conversation until Nate offered tea. At the same time, there was a knock on the door, and Gustav got up to bark. He might not be on top form, but he wasn't going to let a knock go unnoticed.

Nate went out, closing the door behind him. Sam heard muffled voices as she continued to sit with Gustav. The sitting room door opened, and Nate came back in followed by a tall, lean man in his sixties with metal-framed glasses and short, greying hair.

'Sam, this is Inspector Bob Keld. I used to work with him when I was in the police force. He's handling Kaye's murder. If it is murder, of course.'

'Afternoon, miss. Sorry to disturb you, but I would like to have a quick word with you before you go back to the pub.'

Sam got up to shake hands, feeling amused at being called 'miss'. His grasp was firm and dry, his hand almost cold. 'No problem, Inspector. It's all been a horrible shock. I only met Kaye yesterday, and now she's dead. And in dreadful circumstances, it seems.'

'I know. Sit yourself down, lass. Nate, I think you mentioned something about a cup of tea?'

'I did. I'll put the kettle on,' and Nate tactfully disappeared into the kitchen.

'Now, you say you only met Kaye—Miss Butterworth—yesterday. When was that exactly, and why were you meeting her?'

'I'd arranged to go to her cottage at 2. She's—she was—the illustrator for a series of children's books, and I wanted to talk to her about them. I've just started a new job with the company that publishes them. Actually, Kaye was a founder member and on the Board. I'm in marketing, and I'm working on the marketing plan to see if we can increase sales.'

'I see. You met her as planned? Did she seem all right? Anything strike you as odd?'

'No … ,' said Sam, thinking hard. 'No. But then, I'd only spoken to her once on the phone, and I only met her for the first time yesterday. She's quite brusque, but when she was talking about her drawings, she's much more relaxed. Or was more relaxed. I can't get used to her not being here. She loved her work. And she loved Gustav too.' Gustav gave a little wag of his tail when he heard his name. 'What happened to her? Can you tell me?'

Inspector Keld ignored her questions, asking more of his own. 'What time did you leave the cottage? Did you notice anyone nearby?'

'About 4, maybe a bit later. It was dark by then. No, there was no one in the lane. Well, if there was, I didn't see them. I've hurt my ankle and I was concentrating on walking. Oh!' Sam stopped.

'Yes?'

'It's probably nothing.'

'Or it could be something. Tell me, please.'

Chapter Six

Sam wriggled uncomfortably in her armchair, making the leather squeak slightly. Gustav's ears pricked. It felt as though she was telling tales, but Keld was waiting.

'I did see a car. A dark-coloured Nissan Qashqai, maybe black. It was going quite fast. I just got a glimpse of the driver. A man, I think. No passenger.'

'Recognise him?'

'Er, not really.'

'But you have a theory?'

'Well—this really is just a thought that I had at the time.'

'Yes, I understand. Go on.'

'Well, it looked like Brendan. Brendan McManners.'

'And who is Brendan McManners?'

'He runs the publishing company, Little Bear. He's my boss. And Kaye's nephew. But I'm sure he's back in Lower Rushford, in Oxfordshire, where the office is.'

'Not that far away if you have a good car.'

'No. He didn't mention he was coming here though. I told him on Wednesday that I was leaving the next day to meet with Kaye. Surely he would have said if he'd planned to visit her while I'm here?'

'A spur of the moment thing, perhaps. How did he get on with his aunt? Did you pick up on any disagreements?

'I don't know. I don't think they were close. Brendan never referred to her as his aunt, or at least, not to me. You probably don't know about the threats that have been made to someone in Little Bear?'

'What threats?'

'Well, the word 'murderer' was written on some drawings of him. The last one was stuck over the company logo on the wall in reception—with a knife, and it had 'I'll get you' written on it. The local police are looking in to it.'

'I'll speak to them. Back to the aunt and nephew relationship. Anything else you can think of? Anything come up in your meeting with Miss Butterworth?'

'No, I don't think so. Nothing relevant.'

'Don't worry about whether you think it's relevant. Are you staying at the pub tonight? I'd like to talk to you again in the morning. It'll give you some thinking time.'

'What time do you want to meet?'

'9, please. And I like to be punctual.'

Sam couldn't imagine him being anything else. 'No problem. I'm not a suspect, am I?'

'Not at the moment. Ah, here's the tea. I see you haven't forgotten how I take it, Nate.'

'I let it brew for you. It should be strong enough.'

'I've had an interesting talk with your guest. How do you two know each other?'

Nate gave a quick summary of how he and Sam had met, and that he had gone to the pub that morning to let Sam know of Kaye's death.

'I see. Right, I'll be off now, back to the crime scene. Excellent tea. Nate, I'll need to talk to you later, given that you were the one who found her.'

'I'll be here all evening, so call in when you're ready.'

'I will. I'll see myself out. You'll need to keep hold of that dog.'

Sam and Nate said goodbye to Keld. Sam kept a light hold of Gustav but he didn't move. He seemed settled with her, and soothed by her attention.

'I feel as though I've been grilled,' said Sam, looking tired. 'He's nice enough, but he doesn't miss a trick, does he.'

'He's thorough. Never drops anything he thinks is important. Bit like a dog with a bone.' Gustav's head came up. 'Bone' was definitely in his vocabulary. 'Sorry Gustav, not today,' said Nate.

'Did you work with him for a long time?'

'All the years I was in the police force—about 15 years. I joined not long after university. I didn't know what I wanted to do, and it seemed a good enough option. Not that he was very impressed with my history degree.'

'Enjoy it?'

'The degree or the police work?'

'Both.'

Chapter Six

'Degree was great. Good times. Police work? Well, some of it. A lot of the time it was quite boring, routine stuff. Then you'd get stuff happening with the tourists. Fights, drunken behaviour, you know the sort of thing. Nothing that bad. One or two murders over the years but it was fairly quiet.'

'You weren't tempted to write detective stories, then?'

'No. I wanted a complete break. My, um, my wife was in the same police force.'

'Oh! Does she still work for them?'

'No, not now. She, she, er, well, she died.'

'I'm so sorry. That must have been very hard.'

'It was. Still is, although it was a few years ago now.' His expression was closed, not inviting any further comment or questions.

Sam let the silence hang, and said 'I should probably be getting back to the pub.'

'You're welcome to stay here for a bit if you want.'

'No, I'll leave you in peace. I think Gustav is a bit more settled now. And Inspector Keld will want to talk to you at some point.'

'True. All right. Do you want to borrow the book? Have something to take your mind off things?'

'I'd like that. I'll be in the pub this evening if you want to come along for a drink, once you've spoken to the Inspector.'

'That would be nice. Let's see how the evening works out.'

Sam, wrapped up against the cold wind, walked slowly along the lane, thinking back to the car she'd seen last night. She should have asked Jen what car Brendan drove. She'd do that back at the pub, and perhaps Jen would have replied to her earlier text.

Having declined Sandra's offer of sandwiches, Sam slowly made her way upstairs to her room. Her ankle was improving, but a walk was still out of the question. She decided to put her feet up, catch up with text messages, and start thinking about her marketing plan. And of course, she needed to think through the last few days at Little Bear to see if there was anything she should tell Inspector Keld. Her ankle might get a rest, but her brain would not.

First, the text messages. One from her mother. Another from Jen. She tapped to open it and read:

OMG! Dead? How? Very sad. Melissa here yesterday, demanding to know where Brendan was. Yes, Enid and Frank were an item. Is that important?

So, Enid and Frank *were* in a relationship, and clearly some people, even if not everyone at Little Bear knew that. Stacey Barber, who took over Frank's role, didn't seem to know—and if she did, probably wouldn't have felt it necessary to say anything. What did it all mean—if anything?

Where is B? What car does he drive?

Jen replied. *A black Nissan thing. Got a funny name. He's not here.*

A black Nissan with a funny name, thought Sam. *And he's not at work. I'll have to tell Inspector Keld. It all fits. He would have told Kaye about the opportunities in China, shown her the drawings, and told her that sales in the UK had crashed. She'd never agree to selling to China, and Brendan would have got mad. He's not a man to take rejection well. Did he mean to kill her? Nate said she was lying on the floor. Perhaps she had a stroke or a heart attack, brought on by arguing with Brendan? Surely he didn't deliberately murder her?* She shivered slightly, trying to shake off the thought that she'd been employed by someone capable of killing his aunt so his business would prosper.

What about the relationship between Brendan and Kaye? He'd stuck up for her when Melissa declared that the fall in sales were partly because of Kaye's drawings. He'd described her as an 'eccentric old bat'. Sam still winced at that, but it didn't mean he hated her. After all, she was a founder member of the company that had provided him with an income all his life. No, she couldn't point to any evidence of bad feeling between them. Given their strong personalities they were unlikely to get along without a few fireworks, but that didn't mean Brendan had killed her.

Raking over the past week wasn't giving her any answers. She decided to look over her notes for the marketing plan. Once the news got out about Kaye, *Granny Fi* would be in the media and Little Bear would have to be prepared for that. In fact, she realised, *she* would have to be prepared, as, given the size of the company, PR/Communications would probably sit with Marketing as there was no one specifically employed for PR. It was not a welcome thought.

A couple of hours passed as Sam worked steadily. Feeling hungry, she decided to head down to the bar to find out what Sandra was cooking.

She could hear a low buzz of voices from the bottom of the stairs. She pushed open the door to the bar, and looked around for a spare table. She was in luck, but she was glad she had come down early as there was quite a crowd of customers. Judging from their clothing, they were in the area for walking. Wearing fleeces in various bright colours they looked like a flock of exotic birds. There was no break in their chatter as she eased her way through to the bar to order a glass of wine and a meal.

Sipping her wine, Sam couldn't help looking up every time the pub door opened, hoping Nate would look in. It was probably too early. Her lasagne arrived, smelling delicious. She'd just finished eating when Nate arrived. He waited at the bar to order his drink and another glass of wine for Sam. Finally sitting down at Sam's table, she thought he looked tired.

'What a day!' he said.

'It certainly is. I keep thinking about Kaye. It must be much worse for you.'

'Maybe. Anyway, I've talked through everything with Keld so that's out of the way.'

'Does he think it's murder?' asked Sam.

'Unexplained death. In other words, he's not ruling out foul play. He'll know more when he's got the autopsy report.'

'Oh no, poor Kaye.'

'I know. Don't think about it,' advised Nate, taking a few good sips of his beer. 'How was your afternoon?'

'Oh, I've been thinking about what I need to tell the Inspector tomorrow, and getting some work done. Brendan's not in the office.'

'Brendan? Who's Brendan?' Nate asked.

'Oh, he's my boss. I thought he'd be in the office but he's not.

Sorry, I'm rambling a bit,' said Sam, remembering she shouldn't tell Nate anything before she'd told Keld. Nate looked puzzled. 'Let's talk about something else,' suggested Sam. 'What are you writing about at the moment?'

'Are you sure you want to know? Once I start talking about that I tend to go on a bit. I don't want to bore you.'

'I think I'll cope,' said Sam. 'Talk away! As long as it doesn't involve any bodies.'

'No bodies. OK then, don't say I didn't warn you,' and Nate launched into an overview of his current book. His enthusiasm was obvious, and Sam watched his face light up as he talked about the things that mattered to him. She asked a few questions, but mostly let him talk. It was probably doing them both good. Eventually he paused, and she offered to get another round of drinks.

'Better not, I need to get home and see to Gustav. But thanks for listening.'

'I enjoyed it,' said Sam. 'Maybe see you around tomorrow. I'm going back in the afternoon, all being well.'

'Why don't you call in after you've met with Keld? You might need a coffee, and some Gustav therapy.'

'Good idea. Thanks, I'll do that. I can give you the poles back, and your book.'

He really was nice, Sam thought as she went up to her room. It was good to feel she had made a friend, and a male one too, without the complications of feeling attracted. She'd put any thought of a new relationship behind her when she finally plucked up the courage to leave Jack.

Snuggling under the warm duvet she thought the evening had made a good end to a difficult day. Sleep overtook her.

Nate pulled his scarf more closely around his neck and chin, feeling the chill of the wind after the warmth of the pub. He'd enjoyed the evening. The shock of Kaye's death hit him afresh, and the image of her still body lying by the hearthstone floated before his eyes. He blinked it away, and tried to think about the welcome Gustav would give him when he got home. Instead, Sam's face, one moment serious, the next alight with a smile, came into his mind. He found himself hoping he would see her again tomorrow. Quickening his pace, he soon reached his cottage. Gustav gave a quiet bark as he turned the key to unlock the door. Exhaustion hit him, and he quickly took Gustav out for a short walk before heading for bed.

Chapter Seven

Sunday, January 23rd

Sam woke to rattling windows, and what sounded like stones hitting the panes. She got up, wincing slightly as she put her weight on her injured ankle. It was better than yesterday, but still not great. Pulling the curtains slightly apart, she realised it was pouring with rain with a gusting wind, and it was not yet daylight. Disappointing, but not surprising given it was January in Cumbria. Sam looked at her phone. 7.15. She'd take a leisurely shower and then go down for breakfast. She felt surprisingly hungry.

After a good helping of fluffy, buttery scrambled eggs and coffee, Sam felt she could face Inspector Keld. Sandra offered her the use of the bar area as no one else would be in there at nine in the morning. There was a knock on the door, and Sam opened it to find Keld, his waterproofs dripping.

'Good morning, Inspector.'

'Morning, miss. Not a very good one today.'

Sam raised her eyebrows enquiringly, but he indicated the weather. She was relieved there was nothing more to worry about than wind and rain.

'Come through to the bar. Sandra says we won't be disturbed.'

The Inspector took off his dripping waterproofs and hung them over a couple of bar stools. There was no more small talk as he asked Sam what she could tell him.

'Well, I had a text from one of my colleagues. She mentioned that Brendan wasn't at work yesterday. And it looks as though he drives a black Nissan. She couldn't remember the model, but she said it was a funny name. Qashqai is definitely that. I'm starting to think it really was Brendan I saw the night before last.'

'We'll be following that up. Tell me about your meeting with Miss Butterworth. Give me all the detail you can. Don't worry that it might be irrelevant, or that you're boring me. It's the small things that are often important.'

'OK. I phoned Kaye on ….' And Sam took the Inspector step-by-step through her telephone conversation, and her meeting with Kaye. The Inspector took notes, and asked a question from time to time. Watery sunlight came through the window, and Sam suddenly realised she had been talking for some time.

Sam said 'I don't think there's anything else I can tell you. What's going to happen from here?'

'I'm waiting for the report from forensics, and from the pathologist, and we'll go from there.'

'Was she murdered, do you think? I just can't imagine Brendan doing something like that.'

'You'd be surprised what people are capable of. In my line of work you learn not to make assumptions.'

'What about a funeral?'

'That can't happen just yet. The timing depends on what's in the reports.'

'Of course. Am I OK to travel home today? I can leave you my contact details.'

'Yes, you can go home, and yes, I'll need your details. I may well be paying a visit to your offices in the next couple of days.'

'What do you need, just my mobile number?'

'That and your home address.'

'OK.' Sam jotted down the details and gave them to the Inspector. 'Until next time, then.'

With the taxi booked for early afternoon, Sam packed her few belongings and headed out along the lane to Nate's, carrying his poles and book. Her ankle was definitely a lot better.

The police tape was still around the entrance to Kaye's cottage, and a police car was parked outside. Sam knocked at Nate's door, and she heard Gustav's barks of warning.

'Come on in,' said Nate as he answered the door. 'Glad it brightened up a bit for you to walk down here.'

'It was a bit grim earlier! Oh, hello Gustav. Yes, I'll make a fuss of you. Just let me through the door,' she said as Gustav tried to wrap himself around her legs.

'I'll make some coffee. How did it go with Keld?'

'Well, I'm allowed home so he can't think too badly of me.'

'That's good—good about not thinking badly of you. Not good that you're leaving. I'll miss our chats at the pub.'

'I'm sure I'll be back. There'll be Kaye's funeral at some point.'

'True.' Nate sat down, and ran his hand through his hair. 'I'm not too good at funerals, to be honest.'

'No—oh no, of course not,' said Sam, remembering about his wife. 'You don't have to go. There are other ways to remember someone.'

'I'll think about it later. Right, coffee. What time's your train?'

'It's this afternoon. I've got a taxi booked to take me to the station.'

'I could have taken you.'

'You've done more than enough already. I brought your poles back, and your book. I didn't get much of a chance to read it, but I'll definitely try to find a copy when I'm home.'

Jack Henshaw took a slow drive through Lower Rushford. Officially, he was keeping an eye on the locals, although Sunday evenings were usually quiet. But he couldn't get out of his head the information Balinski had shared about Sam. Earlier in the evening, Jack had found the Little Bear offices but of course there was no one there on a Sunday, which left him trawling the streets in the forlorn hope of seeing her and finding out where she now lived. She had no business living anywhere else: she belonged to him, and he had not agreed to her leaving. He wanted her back where she belonged. He'd tried dating other women, but for some reason he hadn't got much attention on the dating apps. And he hadn't seen anyone that appealed to him. It had to be Sam.

Driving slowly through town, he turned off into an area of newer housing. He could not believe his luck: surely that was Sam, with some luggage. Clearly, she'd been away for the weekend! Who had she gone away with? Or perhaps she'd met up with someone? How dare she! She should be at home with him. He followed her at a distance, pulling up as she reached her front door. He noted the number and street name.

The journey back had been long but uneventful. Sam was glad to get off the train and to head home. Rummaging for her door keys, she was aware of a car pulling up on the road behind her. A car door slammed, and she heard footsteps getting closer. She turned, to see Jack Henshaw, her ex-partner, striding towards her.

'What the hell are you doing here?' Sam asked.

'Thought I'd see where you're hanging out. Haven't seen you for a while.'

'No. We split up, remember?'

'So we did. Well, you walked out, as I recall. Why was that, again?'

'I'm not going through that again. I don't want you outside my house.'

'Ask me in then. I'll say yes,' Jack replied, grinning in the way Sam had once found so endearing.

'This is my house. My home. Not yours. I left because I wanted to get you out of my life. Now get lost,' said Sam.

'That's not very friendly.'

'It's not meant to be. I'll say it again: get lost.'

'Ooh, hoity-toity. All right then. Now I know where you are, I might call round another day. Perhaps you'll be feeling friendlier then. And you can tell me all about your weekend away. Who was the lucky bloke, by the way?' leered Jack.

'That's none of your business. You're out of my life, and you can stay out,' said Sam. Jack must have picked up on the fury in her voice because he turned away without saying anything more.

Sam watched him saunter back to his car, and waited until he'd got in. *What arrogance!* she thought as she turned away to avoid seeing if had the cheek to wave. Closing her front door behind her, her legs started trembling as the adrenalin drained away. Sitting down abruptly on the sofa, Sam gave a sob of relief. How could she have thought she had escaped from him so easily?

Her mind immediately started to replay past rows and behaviours. She recalled her fear that she was losing her mind when in fact it was her self-belief she was losing, worn down by Jack's put-down comments and complaints about her neediness and insecurity. With her last scrap of willpower and determination, she had left him. To say he hadn't taken it well was an understatement.

She hadn't told him where she was moving, or about her new job. None of her friends would have told him. Suddenly she remembered Krystof Balinski recognising her. He worked in the same office as Jack. It all fell into place. How easily she had been discovered. Sam suddenly felt tearful, but she blinked away the tears.

She was not going to think about it anymore. Jack Henshaw was no longer a part of her life, and she was going to make sure it stayed that way. She set about unpacking her bag, texting her mother, and getting something to eat. By the time she sat down with a bowl of steaming soup (tinned, but sometimes it had to be done) and a glass of wine she felt a little more relaxed. She had found the courage to stand up to Jack when she left him, and she would face him again if she had to.

Chapter Eight

Monday, January 24th

As soon as she spun through the revolving doors to enter the Little Bear offices, Sam knew that something had happened. There was an oppressiveness to the atmosphere, and not even Debbie could raise a smile. By the time she reached the first floor she could hear a buzz of excited conversation.

'What's happened?' asked Sam.

One of the editors said 'There's a rumour that Kaye's dead, and that Brendan's been arrested!'

'What!' Sam wondered if she should confirm the rumour about Kaye, or whether should she keep quiet. She decided to wait.

'Jason was supposed to have a call with Kaye this morning, but when he phoned the police answered, and said she had died. What were the police doing in her house?' asked a woman Sam didn't yet know.

'And Debbie was walking to work this morning when she saw a police car outside Brendan's house, and he was getting into it with two police officers!' added someone else.

'Perhaps he was just going to talk to the police about Kaye's death?' suggested Sam.

'Hmm, maybe. But that would only happen if her death was suspicious, wouldn't it?'

The speculation continued. Sam's phone rang, and she heard Debbie's voice, telling her that Inspector Keld was already here and would like to see her. She quietly went downstairs to meet him at reception.

'Ah, Miss Holliday. Is there somewhere we can talk?' asked the Inspector, with his usual disregard for any social pleasantries. Sam led him to the office where she'd had her interview with Krystof Balinski.

'We've taken McManners in for questioning. The report came through from the pathologist and all indications are that we cannot rule out that Miss Butterworth was murdered.' He paused as he saw the shocked expression on Sam's face.

'I know, this is difficult for you. I'm still waiting for forensics to get back to me. I'm going to brief the staff here, but I wanted to tell you first. You may find there's media interest—it never takes them long to sniff out a breaking story. I know it's not what you want to think about at the moment but someone in the company should have something prepared.' Sam nodded.

The Inspector pressed on, saying 'I'll need to interview you formally as you were in the vicinity at the time of the murder. I've got confirmation of when you returned to the pub, but I need a statement about your movements that evening. We can do that here — now, if you can.'

'Er, OK. Should I have a solicitor? Sorry, this is a lot to take in.'

'I'm not arresting you. I simply need a statement. It's a formality. If you can do it now, I'll call in one of my colleagues to sit in with me, and it will all be over and done with.'

'OK, let's go ahead then,' said Sam rather more calmly than she felt. 'And I should probably talk to one of the Board about getting prepared for the media—that's Tony Pearson or Clive Frobisher.'

'You can do that after I've finished interviewing you,' replied Keld.

Chapter Eight

Keld went to find his constable, and a tape recorder. Sam tried to get her thoughts in order, anticipating the questions. By the time the Inspector returned with a young constable in tow, she felt a little calmer. The recording underway, the Inspector took her through her last evening in Upper Braithwaite.

'I'd appreciate it if you didn't talk about any of this to your colleagues,' said Keld.

'Of course not,' said Sam, feeling slightly guilty about telling Jen that Kaye had died.

Back at her desk, Jen soon spotted her and demanded news. Sam, speaking quietly, said 'Not here. Can you come to my place for supper, around 6?'

'Can do. By the way, we're all summoned to a briefing at 10.'

The meeting room felt different from the previous briefing with DS Balinski. It was the same group of people, but without Brendan's scowling presence everyone looked more worried than scared. Entering the room, Inspector Keld's seniority and formal manner reinforced the sombreness of the meeting.

'Good morning. I'm Inspector Keld, normally based in Cumbria. I'm here to brief you on recent events which affect all employees of this company. It is my sad duty to inform you that Kaye Butterworth, a member of your Board and a children's book illustrator for Little Bear, was found dead, two days ago, at her home in Upper Braithwaite.' There were several gasps, and people shuffled uneasily, sensing there was more bad news to come.

The Inspector continued. 'We are treating her death as suspicious. The pathologist's report confirms that Miss Butterworth's injuries, which caused her death, may have been inflicted deliberately by another person or persons. In short, it is feasible that Miss Butterworth was murdered.'

The gasps were louder, and there were a few exclamations of 'no' from around the table. Looking around, Sam saw how shocked everyone looked. But not everyone was there: Clive Frobisher, Tony

Pearson, and Enid Price were all missing. *Perhaps they were briefed separately,* thought Sam.

'We are, of course, doing all that we can to discover what happened, and to find the person or persons who committed this heinous crime. I have briefed the remaining members of your Board —Mr Frobisher and Mr Pearson—separately, and they will be talking to you later today.'

'Where is Brendan McManners?' asked Stacey Barber.

'Mr McManners is helping us with our enquiries,' replied the Inspector. 'Now, I realise this is a shock for you all, but I have work to do. Any more questions? No? Good morning to you,' and he quickly left the room.

Everyone started talking at once. Most were disbelieving. Some were concerned about what would happen now that Kaye was dead. No one voiced any concerns about Brendan, or queried Inspector Keld's reference to Brendan 'helping' with police enquiries. A few minutes later, Clive and Tony appeared, and all talking immediately stopped.

'I'm sure you're all saddened at the news of Kaye's death,' said Tony. 'Clive and I have been talking to Mrs McManners, Kaye's sister. The police and her family are with her. Now we need to brief you on what happens here. We're expecting media interest so if you get a call from them, you are not to answer any of their questions. You should direct them to me.

'You are not to talk about Kaye's death to anyone: not to your partner, your friends, your mother, your cat. No one, outside of the office. We will put out a statement for booksellers, and for the media. We already have an obituary written for Kaye, and we will be working on plans to commemorate her great contribution to children's literature in due course. It is too soon to say what her death will mean for the *Granny Fi* series, or for the business. Does anyone have any questions, or shall we all get back to work now?'

Work? After everything we've just heard? Sam thought. She caught Jen's eye: she didn't look convinced either. A few people expressed their shock and sorrow at the news, and there were a few questions that Clive and Tony quickly dealt with. The meeting ended, and everyone drifted back to their desks, unsure what to do next.

'Sam, would you take this call? It's Melissa. Tony and Clive aren't answering, and Brendan's not here, of course. Would you mind?' asked Debbie. She sounded flustered.

'OK, put her through,' said Sam with more confidence than she felt. 'Good morn . . .,' but Melissa wasn't in the mood for pleasantries.

'What the hell is going on? Where is everyone? No one is taking my calls. Who are you?'

'I'm Sam Holliday, the new Marketing Manager. We met last Monday when you came here for a meeting.'

'Oh, you. The one who's going to come up with a marketing plan. That'll all change now of course, with Kaye's death. Could be good for sales. It will get the series in the media, and that might pique people's interest in the books again.'

'Er, yes, I suppose that could happen.' *This woman is unbelievable,* thought Sam.

'So what is going on there? And how do you plan to make the most of the news?'

'We've just been briefed by the Inspector, and Tony Pearson. We'll be putting a statement together for the media. I'm afraid I don't know any more than that.'

'Humph,' snorted Melissa, unimpressed. 'How's the marketing plan shaping up?'

'It's coming along well, but as you said, I'll need to review it given the breaking news.'

'Well, keep me posted. You can count on me for any interviews. I am, after all, the creator of the books that made Kaye's name, not to mention Little Bear's. Where is Brendan?

'I assume he's with his mother. Tony told us her family were with her. I expect other people are in meetings. Do you want me to pass any messages on to anyone in particular?'

'Just that we must optimise what's happened. And I'm available for interview.'

Sam ended the call, and sighed heavily. She should go and talk to Tony, to find out what was happening about the statement to the media.

Climbing the stairs to Tony's office, Sam could hear voices. She paused near the top, uncertain of what she should do.

'Nice move implying Brendan was with his mother.' That was Clive's voice. 'How much longer can we fob her off though? She'll work it out sooner or later. We've no idea how long they'll hold Brendan.'

'There's a limit, I think.' That was Tony. 'Twenty-four hours or something like that.'

'We can't keep telling his mother he's popped out, or he's in a meeting, for much longer. She simply won't believe it. She'll expect him to support her. She has just lost her sister, after all.'

'Does she know it's murder?' asked Clive.

'No. Want to tell her?'

'No, of course not. Oh, God, what a mess. We'll have Cheung on the phone next. Not to mention …'

'Keep your voice down, man! Have you paid that invoice yet?'

'Yes, out of the other account. Do you think the books are safe?

'Not sure. We might need to move them. Got a plan?'

'I can find a man with a van. They're all in boxes so no one going to see what's in them.'

There was a pause before Clive continued. 'What shall we do about the statement Keld said we should prepare?'

'I'll get that marketing woman onto it. Keep her busy, and hopefully that will keep her nose out of things,' said Tony.

Sam retreated quietly down a few stairs, coughed loudly, and went slowly back up. The voices had stopped by the time she reached Tony's door. She knocked, and opening the door said 'Hi, Tony. I'm so sorry about Kaye. It must be a terrible shock—oh, good morning, Clive. Tony, I wondered if you needed me to work on the statement for the media?'

Tony cleared his throat. Clive stood up, nodded curtly at Sam, and said 'I'll be in my office if you need me, Tony.'

'Actually,' said Tony, 'Clive and I were just saying it would be helpful if you could write a statement for the press. Keep it simple, focus on what Kaye meant to Little Bear, and to her readership, you know the sort of thing. You can base it on the draft obituary—I'll send that through to you. Just add a bit about the police investigating the cause of death, and how sad we all are: end of an era, blah, blah.'

Sam nodded. 'Melissa called. She thinks the news about Kaye could help sales. Oh, and she's up for any interviews.'

Tony groaned. 'That woman! She'd sell her own grandmother—in fact, that's probably what she's been doing all these years with her *Granny Fi* books! OK, let's see if anyone asks for an interview. Not that I'm sure I really want to let Melissa lose on the press right now.'

'I'll get on with the statement. I'll email you the draft in the next hour. By the way, I'm not a PR expert. You might want to think about getting some advice on handling media interest,' said Sam.

Tony looked up, surprised. 'We just need a press release. The media can use that. There's nothing more to tell them.'

'Unless they hear about what's been happening with the threats, or the fall-off in sales,' said Sam.

'The only way they'll get hold of that if is someone blabs. And no one is going to do that. Not if they want to keep their job,' said Tony, looking stern.

'Fine, I'll get on to it,' said Sam, glad to get back to her desk. Passing Brendan's office, she thought she'd say hello to Enid, but she wasn't at her desk. The photo with Frank McManners was still by the phone, but the papers with the draft email and illustration had gone.

Sam sat at her desk, staring at her blank laptop screen and the unrelenting flashing of the cursor. Her head was full of the conversation she had just overhead. What invoice did they mean? Could it be the one for printing the latest *Granny Fi* book? What did they mean about the 'other account'? What books were potentially unsafe? She didn't have the answers. She had to push it all to the back of her mind and get the press statement written.

A new email dropped into her inbox with the obituary for Kaye. She read it through a few times, then started to draft the press release. After a few attempts, Sam felt she had a draft that was good enough. She attached it to an email to Tony, hit send, and headed out for some fresh air.

Seeing the shops reminded her that she'd invited Jen for supper, and that she needed to shop. She decided to keep the meal simple—pasta, salad, fruit. She had wine in the fridge. Carrying her supplies, she ignored the temptation of coffee at Gino's, and went back to the office with a heavy heart.

The afternoon dragged on. Trudging back through the quiet streets, she yearned for the quiet cosiness of her home. Jack Henshaw was not going to get a toe over her doorstep, not ever. It would be a violation of everything she had created for herself.

Lost in thought, she arrived at her front door without noticing anything of the walk home. Inside, she quickly dealt with her shopping, laid the table, and got out the wine glasses. Tempting as it was to have a glass now, she decided to wait for Jen.

Jen looked exhausted. She fell gratefully onto Sam's sofa, and accepted the offer of wine.

'I'm so glad you're back,' she said. 'It's been a nightmare.'

'Talk or eat first?' asked Sam.

'Let's eat. Otherwise this wine will go to my head.'

The pasta was soon ready, and soon eaten.

'Wow, that was great,' said Jen, mopping up the rest of her sauce with some crusty bread.

'Make yourself comfy on the sofa, and I'll get the wine for a top up. We've got a lot of talking to do!' said Sam. 'You first. What's been going on here?'

'Oh, loads! Where do I start? Well, you know the makeup bag and the nail varnish are Melissa's? She was absolutely furious about it all, even though the police don't seem to think she used it on the drawings. You would have thought she'd been charged with murder, not just questioned about her nail varnish!'

Sam nodded. 'I can imagine that. One of the few situations where she wouldn't want to be the centre of attention!'

Jen smiled ruefully. 'You're right about that. Anyway, the police asked me to put back those couple of drawings of Brendan that I'd found at the back of my drawer. They wanted me to make it easier for someone to find them, but without being obvious about it. They haven't given me any details about what they're going to do but I'm sure they're using the drawings to set a trap. Nothing's happened yet though, or not that I've heard. Melissa's been a nightmare, as I said. Nothing new there, but she's taken it to a whole new level. Anyway, she's gone home now. Everyone's worried, and a bit scared.' Jen paused to take a sip of wine. 'So, what happened with Kaye?'

Sam talked about her visit, and seeing Kaye's early illustrations. She talked about the pub, and twisting her ankle, and briefly about meeting Nate. She talked about the shock of hearing that Kaye was dead. Jen listened intently.

'Did you think it was murder?'

'I didn't see the body,' said Sam carefully.

'You know more, don't you? But you can't say,' Jen said with some disappointment. 'OK, I get it, if the police have told you to keep quiet, then that's what you have to do.'

Sam had known Jen for barely a week, but instinctively she trusted her. Sam took a deep breath.

'Jen, I think there's something odd going on.'

Jen looked at her enquiringly over the top of her wine glass. 'Well, none of this is exactly normal, even for Little Bear,' said Jen.

Sam gave her a quick smile and continued. 'The invoice for the latest *Granny Fi* book wasn't paid. Stacey was worried about it. And the stock's disappeared into a black hole. The bookseller I called hadn't seen the book. And today—well, today, I overhead a really weird conversation.' She paused. Should she go on? Yes. She had to talk this through.

'I heard Tony and Clive talking. They mentioned another

account, and paying an invoice from it. And Tony asked if the books would still be safe. I don't know what to make of it.'

'What?' asked Jen. She paused with her glass raised midway to her mouth. 'Another account? And what books?'

'I don't know, I just don't know.' Sam stood up, and poured herself another glass of wine. 'I saw an invoice on Clive's desk last week. It was from a printer in China. Clive told me he didn't know if the invoice for the new *Granny Fi* books had been paid or not. But surely he'd know? It would be for a quite a lot of money.'

'I would have thought he'd know. There's an authorisation process for payments. But this other account—is it just an account, or another company? If it's a company, it would have to be registered, assuming it's a limited company, of course. You can check online, with Companies House.'

'Yes! Of course! Hang on, I'll just get my phone.' Sam keyed in her query, and soon the information from Companies House appeared. 'There are two companies: Little Bear, with Brendan, Tony, Clive, Frank, Mrs McManners and Kaye as directors. And another one: Big Bear, with Brendan, Tony, and Clive. Big Bear hasn't registered any trading figures—oh, it only got set up nine months ago.'

'So, the invoice could have been paid through Big Bear. But why?' asked Jen.

'I don't know. It doesn't feel right though, does it? And another thing, Clive wasn't at all keen for me to access the sales figures. He fobbed me of with some IT problem, and that he'd ask the IT guy to set up access for me. I went with it at the time, but now ...'

'Could any of this have anything to do with Kaye? I mean ... could she have been involved?' asked Jen.

'I didn't know her for very long, just that one meeting, but I'd stake my life on Kaye being honest. She wouldn't have colluded in any kind of dodgy practices.'

'I agree. I didn't know her well either, but she seemed very straightforward.'

'So where does this leave things?'

'Still waiting to see if anyone takes the bait of the drawing. And whether the police hold Brendan for any longer. Who killed Kaye. There's just so much going on ….'

'I know,' said Sam. 'We can't solve it tonight. Let's see what happens tomorrow. Perhaps we'll start getting some answers. For now, though, I've got to get some sleep.'

Jen took the hint and got up to get her coat. 'Thanks for suggesting this, Sam. And for cooking. I know it's really difficult at the moment, but it's been just the evening I needed.'

'No problem. I'll walk part of the way back with you. I could do with some fresh air before I turn in.'

Going their separate ways at the bridge, Sam decided to walk the long way back to her house. It was a clear, cold night, and she was enjoying the quiet. Behind the curtains of people's sitting room windows, lights glowed softly. Everything looked so normal.

She passed a high drystone wall, and through the gate glimpsed a large property that could be a barn conversion. Suddenly, she smelt smoke, and saw the bright glow of fire. This was no wood-burning stove: part of the property was on fire. As she looked, she saw a figure move quickly across the garden to a small side gate. Head down, the figure came through the gate, out onto the pavement, scurrying along as though there wasn't a minute to lose. They hadn't seen Sam who was just pulling out her phone to call the emergency services.

'Oh!' said the person as they collided with Sam. 'Oh! It's you!'

'Enid?' said Sam. 'Enid, what are you doing here?'

'Oh, I was just posting something through Brendan's door.'

'This is Brendan's house?'

'Yes, it is.'

'But … but, it's on fire!'

'Is it really?' asked Enid. Sam sensed a hint of a smile in her voice.

Sirens sounded in the distance, the volume increasing as a police car followed by a fire engine screeched to a halt outside Brendan's main gate. DS Krystof Balinski and DC Meera Chaudhury got out of the police car and ran over to Enid.

'Move away, Sam!' Sam instinctively did as she was told. 'Enid

Price,' continued Balinski 'I am arresting you for intent to murder, and to harm property. You do not have to say anything, but it may harm your defence if you do not mention when questioned something which you later rely on in court. Anything you do say may be given in evidence either during your arrest or before questioning.'

Enid staggered, and Balinski put out an arm to steady her. 'I have to handcuff you,' he said.

'No, no,' moaned Enid. 'It's not me who's the murderer—it's him,' she said, trying to point at the house.

'Is it really necessary to handcuff her?' asked Sam.

'Yes,' he snapped. 'Stand aside, before I arrest *you* for preventing the police from carrying out their business.'

Sam hurriedly stood back. It was as though she had stepped into a different world. Gone was the quiet side street, and in its place was a noisy road where large vehicles had stopped with engines running and blue lights flashing. She hadn't had chance to put through a 999 call. Perhaps a neighbour had seen the smoke and called the fire service.

The main gate to Brendan's house was now open, and fire fighters moved purposefully between the fire engines and the house. Other fire crew were starting to roll out the hoses. Voices added to the hubbub, as the fire fighters worked to assess the situation, and what they would need to do. One fire fighter walked over to where Sam was standing with the police and Enid.

'Evening. Were any of you in the premises when the fire started? Or do you know if it's likely anyone is inside?' asked the firefighter of the group. From his white hat and his commanding manner, he was clearly in charge of the fire crew.

'We've reason to suspect this person was in the vicinity,' said Balinski, indicating Enid.

'What can you tell me about the property?' asked the fire fighter.

'Nothing,' spat Enid.

'Don't make things worse for yourself. If you know people are in there, tell us now,' said Balinski.

'Yes, you must, and quickly!' confirmed the fire officer.

Enid hesitated.

Chapter Eight

'Come on, Enid. Who could be in there?' asked Sam as gently as she could. Enid looked at her.

'No one. Brendan's out somewhere, and he lives on his own.'

'Brendan McManners?' asked Balinski. Enid nodded. Balinski turned to the fire officer and told him 'The owner is staying with us at the moment, and has been since this morning,' added Balinski.

Enid looked bewildered.

'Ah, I see,' said the fire fighter. 'Any idea where the fire started, or how it started?'

Enid's whole body seemed to sag. 'It's the garage, not the house. It's lighter fuel. The stuff you use for BBQs. It was on the floor of the garage.'

'Any idea what else is in the garage?'

'Books. Boxes and boxes of books. They should have been in the bookshops. He's a thief! And a murderer! He killed my Frank! He deserves to die!' Enid's face was screwed up with fury. Her head-scarf had slipped, her hair escaping into wild tendrils. She looked a mess, and, thought Sam, completely mad.

'Right, that's very helpful,' the fire fighter told Enid, seemingly unphased by her violent accusations. Walking briskly through the gate and towards the house, he updated his crew. It was now obvious that the garage was the centre of the blaze.

Sam watched as Enid's hands were handcuffed behind her back, and DC Chaudhury walked her to the car. Enid struggled to get onto the back seat, finding it awkward without the use of her arms. *Enid, what have you done*? Sam wondered.

Balinski turned to Sam. 'Any idea what she meant by all that?'

'I think so. I think you'll find copies of the latest book in the *Granny Fi* series were stored in Brendan McManners' garage. Enid's right, they should be in bookshops and people should be buying them. But they went missing. I've no idea why she thinks he murdered Frank—that's Brendan's brother, by the way. Frank died of a heart attack on the stairs of the Little Bear offices, a few months ago.'

'OK. Well, I'll see if the fire crew can salvage any books as evidence. Valuable, are they?'

'Yes, they are the latest book in a series that has made millions for Little Bear over many years,' explained Sam quickly.

Balinski nodded, and walked over to talk to one of the fire fighters handling the hoses.

'Should be able to get a few out at least,' said the fire fighter. 'If they're in boxes, it would take some time for the fire to burn through them—the density slows down the burn. They'll be smoke-damaged, so they'll smell of course.'

'No problem. Just get what you can.' Balinski looked over to Sam. 'Don't hang around here. Go home. I'll be at your office in the morning, and I'll speak to you then.' He got in the car, and Sam watched sadly as Enid was driven away.

Inspector Keld yawned loudly, cracked his knuckles, and went in search of some tea. Walking across the open-plan office, he saw DS Balinski and DC Chaudhury returning.

'Quiet night?' he asked.

'You're joking!' replied Balinski. Keld looked at him, one eyebrow raised quizzically.

'Anything I should know about?' asked Keld.

Balinski hesitated. He'd much prefer to work on this case without Keld's interference.

'If you know anything that will help my enquiry, you must tell me, son.'

Balinski winced slightly at the 'son'. Keld was right, though. He had to tell him what had happened that evening.

'Let's find somewhere quiet to talk,' said Balinski. He led the Inspector into a small, windowless office and sat down.

'Are you aware that we set a trap at the Little Bear offices?'

'No, I wasn't. What trap, and why?' asked Keld.

Balinski explained about the drawings, with the word 'murderer' written on them.

'Yes, yes, I know about those,' said Keld impatiently.

Chapter Eight

'Whoever was doing this found the drawings in the desk of one of the staff. I'll spare you the details, but we set a trap using the remaining drawings, and we set up CCTV to see what would happen. Now we knew it would have to be someone pretty stupid—or someone so fixated on threatening McManners—to take the bait. But someone did.'

'Who was it?' asked Keld.

'My DC checked the CCTV, and saw Enid Price taking the drawings and then leaving the building. She's Brendan McManners secretary. We were going to talk to Price tomorrow, but DC Chaudhury and I were driving near the Little Bear offices and saw her, scuttling along the pavement and heading for the town. She looked very purposeful, and angry, so I got out of the car to follow her to see what she did.

'And?' prompted Keld.

'I kept some distance away—I didn't want to alarm her, but I saw her turn into a side street and then enter a gateway. I waited a bit further back to see if she'd come out again. I radioed DC Chaudhury to park nearby but out of sight of the house thinking I'd need to get back in the car in a few minutes. I wasn't really expecting anything to happen. I assumed she had arrived at her home. Nothing did happen, so I went closer and looked over the garden gate and saw the start of the fire—well, smoke really. I called up the fire brigade, and then radioed DC Chaudhury to bring the car round to the house. I waited to see if Enid Price would re-appear, and then I saw her run out of the gate, just as Sam Holliday turned up.

'Sam Holliday?' queried Keld.

'Yes, Sam Holliday. She was just on her way home when Price charged out of the gate and nearly flattened her.'

'Sam's OK though?' asked Keld with a frown of concern.

'Fine, as far as I know,' said Balinski. 'I arrested Price, who pretty much admitted to starting the fire. She told us it was Brendan McManners' house. He's in custody here, of course, and from what Price said, she is out for revenge for various crimes she believes he's committed. Anyway, she stinks of BBQ lighter fuel. My car reeks of it too. We brought her back here for questioning. She's in a cell to calm down a bit. Bonkers, I'd say.'

Keld raised his eyebrows. 'A few interesting developments, then. Was it definitely Enid Price who left the other threatening messages? Has she explained why she started the fire?'

'She said McManners was a thief. Apparently, he'd kept boxes of books in his garage which should be in bookshops.'

Keld looked mystified.

'Don't ask me,' continued Balinski. 'She's really lost it. She called him a murderer again—that was the word she scrawled on the drawings.'

'What, she thinks he murdered Kaye Butterworth?' asked Keld.

'No, she thinks Brendan murdered his brother, Frank McManners. 'Her Frank,' she called him,' said Balinski. Keld's eyebrows shot up again.

'*Another* murder?' Keld asked.

'According to Sam Holliday, Frank McManners died of a heart attack. Whether or not his brother did anything to bring that on, I have no idea. Even if he did, it would be almost impossible to prove. especially as this all happened a few months ago,' said Balinski.

'You don't think Sam Holliday is involved at all?'

'No, I'd say Price was working on her own. It was a coincidence that Sam was on the scene this evening, and she seemed upset about the fire, and Price.'

'I'll call her, see if she can throw any light on any of it.'

'She can probably tell you more about the books.'

'Right. I'll let you know if I find out anything useful. I'll leave you to talk to Price,' said Keld as he returned to his desk.

A feeling of both relief and tiredness swept over Sam as soon as she settled on her sofa, cradling a mug of tea, with her legs curled up underneath her. Any hope of some quiet time to recover from the evening's events was dashed by the insistent ringing of her phone.

Chapter Eight

She let it go through to voicemail, and listened as the caller left their message.

'Keld here. I need to talk to you about some developments. Please call me as soon as you get this message.'

Developments? thought Sam. *What developments?* She put her mug down, and immediately called Keld back.

'Hello, Inspector. Sorry not to take your call. I was …'

'Never mind all that. What do you know about boxes of books stored in Brendan McManners' garage?'

'Er, not much. I suspect they are the new *Granny Fi* books. There's a bit of a mystery about them.' Sam gave Keld a quick summary. 'But it's looking as though the books *were* printed, and the invoice was paid from a sister company. It's all a bit confusing.'

'Hmm. The payment's not necessarily illegal, but it is odd. Any idea what's behind all this?'

'No. I'm starting to wonder if Brendan was setting up Little Bear to fail, possibly to start again with different people on the Board. Up until quite recently the company was doing well, staff were given pay rises, and there was talk of renovating the offices but that all went quiet. The next thing that happens is this fall-off in sales.'

'You know Enid Price has been arrested. Why would she want the books destroyed?'

'No idea. She looked quite pleased she'd started the fire though.'

'What has she got against Brendan McManners?'

'She sounded really angry that the books weren't in the bookshops. She called him a thief. And a murderer. She said he killed Frank, his brother. I don't know why she would say that though. Frank McManners died of natural causes. Brendan isn't an easy man, or a very pleasant one. I've only been there just over a week and I can see how scared most people are of him. But murder? That's a big accusation.'

'You say most people are scared of him. Who are the exceptions?' asked Keld.

'The directors, or at least the two who work at Little Bear. They're all related—cousins, I was told,' said Sam.

'The directors being Tony Pearson and Clive Frobisher?'

'Yes. Brendan's brother, Frank, was a director too.'

'You said his death was from natural causes?'

'The woman who took over his job told me he had a heart attack at the top of the stairs, and fell down them. Enid found him.'

'Bit of a shock for her.'

'Yes. Yes ….'

'Go on.'

'It's just that Frank and Enid were in a relationship. She had a photo of him on her desk. It was a group photo. Both Enid and Frank were in it, and they looked quite close. I asked Jen Somerville if they were an item, and she said they were. What if … no, that can't be right …'

'Let's hear it.'

'Maybe Brendan put pressure on Frank about something, and Enid believes that caused the heart attack? Maybe something about printing the new book, and Frank wouldn't do what Brendan wanted? Maybe Brendan pushed Frank down the stairs and he had a heart attack because of that. But why would Brendan need to get Frank out of the way?' Sam realised she was probably over-speculating, and stopped. There was a pause while Keld waited to see if she was going to say anything further.

'What was Frank's job at Little Bear?' he asked.

'Production Director. That meant he was responsible for the getting the books printed.'

'So he would know whether or not these missing books were printed, and about the payment?'

'I would have thought so. The woman who's taken his role, as a Production Manager, not Director, didn't know where the books were printed, or if the printer had been paid, and she didn't know where the stock is either.'

'What's her name?'

'Stacey Barber.'

'Hmm.'

Sam wondered what the 'hmm' meant. Did Keld agree with her line of thought? Or did he know more than he was letting on?

Chapter Eight

'Thank you, Miss Holliday. Once again, you've been most helpful. Good night.'

The phone went dead, and Sam was left looking at her mug of now cold tea and wondering what to do next. The washing up, perhaps? Or perhaps not. She could phone her mother. Definitely not. A bath, and an early night? That sounded more inviting. She could use that expensive-smelling bath oil her mother had given her for Christmas. Herby, fruity aromas, and then her cosiest pyjamas. At this rate she'd soon be thinking about getting a cat, or taking up knitting. On second thoughts, knitting sounded far too demanding.

An hour later, feeling better for the warmth of both bath and pyjamas, Sam slid under the duvet and nestled it around her neck. Her mind started to pick over the events of the day but she was desperate for sleep. Closing her eyes, she focused on her breathing, intending to count sheep but somehow the sheep turned into boxes of books that kept moving up a hill. She had no idea how many there were as she was still counting them as she fell into a deep sleep.

Chapter Nine

Tuesday, January 25th

'It's seven o'clock on Tuesday, 25th January, and it's time for the news with Poppy Carlisle.'

Sam half-listened, half-dozed under her duvet to the soothing tones of Poppy Carlisle reporting on global events and the latest parliamentary scandals.

'Kaye Butterworth, the illustrator of the popular *Granny Fi* books, was found dead at her home in Cumbria earlier this week. The police believe her death was suspicious. Butterworth was co-founder of the highly regarded children's publishing company, Little Bear, which she started over 30 years ago with her sister. Brendan McManners, a company director and Butterworth's nephew, is currently helping police with their enquiries.'

Hells bells! That's not what I put in the press release! Sam reached for her phone. A text from Jen.

Heard the news? Meet u end of ur road @ 8. Will show you back entrance to office. Press will be at front.

Relieved, Sam replied quickly, and started to get ready for work.

She was out the door just before 8, and Jen was already at the end of the road.

'This was a great idea, thanks, Jen.'

Jen smiled a tight smile. 'It's going to be hell. Tony and Clive will be having the jitters, the phones won't stop ringing, and we'll be mugged as soon as we try to leave the premises.'

'Any good news?'

'We can't even escape to Gino's.'

'Pick up a take away on the way in then?'

'Sam, that is the best thing I've heard all morning. You're on. And I don't even care if I'm late for work.'

'Fighting talk!' and the women laughed as they walked quickly towards the café.

Twenty minutes later Sam was no longer laughing. She'd made the mistake of looking down through the open ironwork stairs that zig-zagged up to the top floor of Little Bear's offices.

'You all right?' Jen called from further up. 'Don't look down, you'll get vertigo!'

'Too late, I think I already have,' said Sam in a small voice.

'OK, I'm coming back down.' Sam shuddered at Jen's rapid descent. She could so easily slip, and then she'd fall, and then …

Stop, she said firmly to herself. She breathed out slowly and made herself look at her coffee cup. She took a sip, and then another.

'Are you having a coffee break, or are you coming into work?' Jen asked. Sam wasn't sure if she was annoyed or trying to be funny.

'Sorry, I don't like heights. I'm OK now. If you take it steady, I'll just follow you up. Do we go all the way to the top?'

'You look really pale! Sure you're OK? It's just two more lots of stairs and then we can get in on the second floor. Stay close.'

A few minutes later one of the editorial staff slid back a glass door to admit Jen and Sam.

'Sorry to disturb you,' said Sam, stepping onto a firm floor with some relief.

'You're the eleventh lot so far. I'm thinking of moving on to a career as a doorman,' grinned the editor.

Chapter Nine

Looking out of a window at the front of the building, Jen and Sam could see a few reporters loitering on the pavement outside.

'Hope Debbie's OK,' said Sam. 'I think I'll go down and check.'

Debbie sat hunched over her computer keyboard. She jumped as Sam said 'hi.'

'Oh, hi, Sam. What can I do for you?'

'I came to see if you were OK. I see we've got a few press people outside.'

'Yes. Some of them came in but there was nothing I could tell them so they're waiting for someone to arrive who might give them a titbit of news. Horrible, isn't it?'

'I suppose they're only doing their job, but it can get a bit much. Can you just lock the doors if it gets out of hand?'

'I'm going to do that after 9.30. Most people should be in by then.'

'Call me if I can help with anything,' said Sam as she headed back upstairs to her desk. As she turned the corner, she nearly bumped into Stacey Barber.

'Oh! Sam, I was just looking for you. Got a minute?' and she indicated that Sam should follow her. Once inside Stacey's office with the door closed firmly behind them, Sam asked 'what's up?' Behind the purple-framed glasses, Stacey's eyes had a worried expression.

'Well,' Stacey said. 'I don't know where to begin really, what with all the news yesterday. And now—now I've found something, and I don't know what to do. I don't know why I'm asking you, but I don't really know many people here. And for some reason I feel I can trust you.' As she was speaking, Stacey picked up some large sheets of paper, her hands trembling.

'What is it?' asked Sam, looking at the sheets of paper. They were printer's proofs for a book, and as Sam leant closer, she realised what she was looking at.

'These are proofs for the new *Granny Fi* book, right?'

'Yes, they would have been used to check the book before all the stock was printed. It's a bit unusual to have proofs like this nowadays, but I think Frank was old-school. But it's not the proofs that are the problem, it's what was *with* the proofs.'

Sam looked at her, questioningly. 'What was it?'

'A letter. An open letter. Here, you read it,' and she pushed the letter into Sam's hands.

Sam looked at the page of pale blue notepaper. *Who used notepaper, these days? Or wrote using a fountain pen?* she wondered. Turning over the page, she read Frank McManners signature. Yes, old-school. Nice handwriting, she noticed. Turning the letter over again (there was only the single page), Sam read in growing dismay.

To whom it may concern

If you're reading this, I'm dead. Perhaps you've taken on my job. Be very careful. Not everything here is as it seems. Step out of line, and your fate will be the same as mine.

I was Production Director at Little Bear for over 20 years, loyal to my mother and her sister who started the company. I never felt the same loyalty to my brother, Brendan, or to those other charlatans that he got voted on to the Board. The company started small, but success with a few series made it prosperous. Ripe for a buy-out. And my brother was not going to have that. With our mother and aunt's advancing years, my dear brother was plotting the future he felt he deserved, jumping in to bed with partner publishers in China to grow the company while keeping his power as Chair—or CEO—at Little Bear. No buyout for him. Not even when we were offered a multi-million-pound figure from Harveys plc. The American-owned publishing house. He hated them.

We had to kill the series that made our company so attractive to Harveys. So instead of printing the new Granny Fi book and getting stocks into bookshops as we always did, Brendan asked me to use a different printer in China to get some copies printed on the cheap, and get them all delivered to his home. He'd show copies to his mother and Kaye, and to Melissa. But for the time being, he'd sit on the rest of the stock. Sales would plummet. It was wrong— unethical. We'd lose the buyout offer, and we'd probably lose the company too, or it would have to downsize with everything that would mean for staff. So I refused to obey orders. I reasoned with him, but my brother is beyond reason. He will do anything to get his own way. And I mean anything.

My heart, as Brendan knows only too well, is on borrowed time. Will it be a heart attack, brought on by stress? Or is he deranged enough to kill me? He will want me out of the way—permanently. I'm sorry for Enid. These last few months have been such happy ones, and whatever future I had looked all the brighter with her beside me. I'm sorry, Enid, that I'm not here. Please forgive me.

Yours ever

Frank McManners

Sam looked up, the shock she felt reflected in Stacey's face. 'What the hell do we do now? This is an accusation of murder,' said Sam.

Stacey took the letter from Sam's outreached hand. 'I know. We have to tell the police, don't we?'

'Yes. I've got a number for Inspector Keld—he interviewed me when Kaye was found. I'll call him.' Stacey looked puzzled, and Sam quickly filled her in on her visit to Upper Braithwaite while she looked for Keld's number. One ring, and she heard his gravelly voice answer with the customarily brusque 'Keld.'

'Inspector, it's Sam Holliday,' Sam said as the office door was thrown open, and the phone snatched from her hand. A voice she recognised demanded to know why she was 'bothering the police'. It was Tony Pearson, and he didn't look happy.

'I want an explanation—now. If you've got anything to tell the police about, you tell it to me and Clive first, so we can decide how to handle it for the business. Got it?'

'Yes … yes, I see that. I'd like my phone back, please,' said Sam, quaking inwardly while sounding surprisingly firm. 'I get that you're worried, but you can't just snatch my phone off me.'

Tony looked a little sheepish, and handed back the phone. 'What were you going to tell the Inspector? And what's all this on your desk, Stacey?'

'I was just showing Sam the proofs for the latest book. She hasn't seen the book itself—no one has—and she thought the illustrations might be useful for press releases, or for the marketing plan,' improvised Stacey.

'Humph,' snorted Tony, not looking entirely convinced. Sam looked him straight in the eye and confirmed Stacey's explanation. 'So why the call to Keld?' he asked.

'Er, seeing the proofs reminded me that I'd forgotten to tell him how much Kaye hated drawing bees. He said I was to tell him anything I remembered, however small.'

'Hmm. Sounds to me as though you were wasting his time. But like I said, if there's anything you want to tell the police , you tell me or Clive first. I'll leave you to it,' and he turned to leave.

The two women continued to look at the proofs as they listened to Tony's retreating footsteps.

'What was that all about?' asked Sam. 'You were brilliant, by the way.'

'Thanks. I didn't think we should share Frank's letter with him, do you?'

'Definitely not! Tony and Clive have got to be involved in some way, even if they didn't actually commit murder. I'm not sure if Tony really bought my excuse for phoning Keld though.'

'Tony's got such a poor opinion of anyone who's not in sales, he won't expect you to do anything clever.'

'Ouch! Oh well, that will work in our favour this time then!' and the two women smiled at each across the desk.

'So, you'll call Keld?' asked Stacey.

'I will. I'll go out for an early lunch. Oh god, I'll have to go down those stairs again.'

'What stairs?'

'The ones that go round the back of the offices: the open ironwork ones. They freak me out.'

'Oh no, not nice. I braved the paparazzi, such as there were when I came in at seven.'

'What shall we do about this letter?' There was a pause. 'How about we both photograph it so we've got a copy on both our phones?'

'Good idea. I'm going to put the original in the book I'm

reading. It's in my bag. Then if Tony comes back to rummage around my office, he won't find it. I don't see him being very interested in the latest Booker Prize winner!'

'No, I think it'll be safe! Right, I'll let you know what Keld says. Do you want to give me your mobile number? Then I don't need to come in to your office again.'

Nate sat at the table he used as a desk, laptop open, deep in thought. Gustav was lying next to him, head on Nate's feet. The cursor blinked on the screen but didn't move. Nate had not typed anything for several minutes. Outside the window, the clouds scudded past at a brisk pace, casting shadows on the hillsides. Nate was oblivious. His mind was reliving the moment when he was told his wife had died. Disbelief, horror, outrage, grief, all coursed through him until he reminded himself it had happened five years ago. For a moment, it felt like yesterday. The thought of 'moving on' filled him with dread, although he knew that was what he needed to do. He liked Sam. She was good company, she listened, and he didn't feel she was pushing for more than friendship. Perhaps he could email her, just to ask how she was getting on. He could manage that much.

Sam expected the morning to go slowly, but when she got back to her desk, there was an email waiting for her from Nate.

> Hi Sam,
> I hope you don't mind me trying to contact you. I took a guess at your work email so if I've got it wrong, this might not reach you! But if it does, I just wanted to check in that you're OK. I heard the report of Kaye's murder on the news this morning, and that Brendan is helping with enquiries. Sounds very commendable, but we all know what that really means.

The police have still got Kaye's cottage cordoned off, and Gustav is staying with me. He seems to be settling in but I sense he still misses Kaye. It's early days. I haven't seen anything more of Keld, so he's probably down south with you.

Anyway, if you'd like to stay in touch, you've got my email address. My mobile is 07844 362154 if you want to text or call.

Take care of yourself. Hope your ankle has now fully recovered.

Best wishes

Nate

A kind email from a kind man, thought Sam. She still had the business card he'd given her in the pub, but he must have forgotten he'd given it to her. Would she like to stay in touch? There didn't seem to be any strings attached to his suggestion, just a shared concern with what happened to Kaye, and with Gustav. Yes, she realised, she *would* like to stay in touch, and she'd text him later. She didn't want Tony or Clive peering over her shoulder and questioning why she wasn't focused on her work.

She dealt with a few work-related emails, and opened her marketing plan. She re-read what she'd written when she was at the pub in Upper Braithwaite, making a few changes to take into account recent events. She was immersed in her work when the vibration of her phone made her jump. Six text messages, all from her mother. Of course, Elaine had heard the news. She replied quickly to assure her mother that she was fine, and that she'd phone her later.

At noon, she left her desk and decided to walk out through the front, revolving door. As the door spun round, she could see the reporters ready to pounce on her as soon as she stepped outside. It was a small group, but with their cameras and microphones thrusting towards the doorway they looked quite intimidating. Digging her chin down into her scarf she avoided eye contact with them and focused on shouldering her way through to the pavement. She couldn't dodge the volley of questions though.

'Hey, what do you think about Kaye's murder?'

'Who do you think did it?'

Chapter Nine

'Is he guilty?'

'Is the company about to fold?'

'Expecting to lose your job?'

'No comment, no comment, excuse me, excuse me,' said Sam, as she tried to keep moving through them. *Vultures,* she thought, as she ducked away from the last of the phones, microphones, and cameras pointed in her direction. She kept her expression neutral, trying not to look either worried or annoyed, and felt relieved when she was at last walking freely towards her house. It seemed the best place to call Keld, and she was glad to step into her calm sitting room.

After a short pause, Sam heard the now familiar gravelly voice answer with the customary 'Keld.'

'Inspector, it's Sam Holliday. Is this a good time to talk to you?'

'Yes. I've been expecting you to call back after you got cut off this morning.'

'I'll explain about that in a minute. But I've got something really important to tell you. My colleague, Stacey Barber—I think I mentioned her to you?'

'You did.'

'Well, she showed me a letter she'd just found among some proofs of the new *Granny Fi* books. You know, the books Enid said were in Brendan's garage.'

'Yes, continue.'

'The letter is signed Frank McManners. In the letter he claims that Brendan was putting him under pressure to do something he thought was unethical.'

'Explain,' said Keld. Sam gave him as much detail as she could remember.

'You have this letter?'

'I have a photograph of it on my phone. So does Stacey. And she's got the original. Oh, and Tony heard me about to make a call to you this morning, and demanded that any new information was shared with him or Clive, the other director, first. That's why the call got cut off.'

'I'll have words with them about that. In the meantime, I'd like to get a copy of this letter. Can you send me the photograph of it for now? I will need the original too.'

'Could you pick the original up from Stacey's house? I'll ask her for her address and let you know.'

'Good, we'll do it that way. I'm going back to Cumbria tomorrow.'

'Have there been any further developments?'

'There are a few matters I need to deal with. In fact, it might be useful for you to be there too, in the next few days.'

'Could it be at the weekend? It would be easier with work. I'm too new to take days off.'

'Let me see what needs to be done first, and I'll confirm. If the police need you, your company will have to let you go,' said Keld.

'Right, of course,' said Sam, but Keld had already gone.

Sam dropped her phone onto her sofa and decided she may as well get last night's washing up done while she was here. The familiar task was soothing, and her mind wandered back to Cumbria. If only she could go back there and simply enjoy the countryside.

Sam headed out into the cold to return to work. The crowd of reporters around the entrance was smaller now, and the two or three remaining seemed more half-hearted with their questions. Sam thought how cold and bored they looked: they'd be gone by the time she left for the day. She smiled to herself, just as one of them pushed in front of her and snapped a photo.

Chapter Ten

Wednesday, January 26th

Debbie showed the newspaper and what had come through on her newsfeed to Sam as soon as she stepped into reception. The photo of Sam which the reporters had taken yesterday was on the front page of the local paper, and on the paper's social media. 'Smiling at death: the heartless world of publishing' ran one report. And there was Sam, smiling quietly, not, as the media claimed, at Kaye's death, but at the prospect of leaving the building unhindered by journalists desperate for a story.

'Tony's going ballistic. I'm really sorry, Sam,' said Debbie quietly.

Sam stared at dismay at the media coverage. There was a report about the fire, but not much had been made about the property belonging to Brendan. With no salacious gossip to share, the reporter had seen an opportunity when Sam smiled, and had run with it. *Vultures* was too kind a description, thought Sam. *Hyenas*, perhaps? And she'd only just managed to reassure her mother that she was fine, although yes, work was a bit tricky at the moment.

'OK, thanks for the tip-off, Debbie. I'd better go and see him.'

Sam wearily climbed the stairs to her desk. She'd just taken off her coat when the door burst open.

'You! My office, now!'

'Good morning, Tony,' said Sam, in an attempt to shame Tony into some manners.

'Are you trying to be funny? What in the name of god is *good* about this morning? Oh, but of course, you're the one who *smiles at death.* Well, it's one way to make front page news, I suppose.' Tony turned to go back to his office, throwing his parting shot, 'Enjoying your moment of fame?' over his shoulder.

'Ouch,' said Sam. Jen's head appeared over the workstation partition.

'Ouch indeed. How did all this happen? I thought you were using the outside stairs?'

'I decided to brave the press pack. I was just thinking how cold and bored they looked, and that they'd be gone by the time I finished work. That made me smile to myself, and that's when one of them took the photo.'

'Bad timing. Good luck with Tony. I think you'll just have to let him rant. I'll make a coffee for when you get back to your desk.'

Sam smiled her thanks, and feeling more angry than scared, went up the stairs to Tony's office. She was not going to be intimidated, especially when what had happened was not her fault.

Jen was right: it was almost impossible to get a word in, and even when she did, Tony was in no mood to listen. Sam had no choice but to wait until his outburst ran its course. Rather like waiting for a two-year-old to finish a tantrum, she thought, managing not to smile.

'What do you plan to do from here?' Sam asked when Tony finally paused for breath.

The question was unexpected.

'Do? What do you mean?' he blustered.

'Well, do you want any further press releases? What do you want to do about Melissa? Is there anything I can do to help?'

'Help? Good god, no. You've done more than enough already—and that is not a compliment! Keep your head down. Do whatever it is you marketing people spend your time doing. And keep Melissa quiet.'

'Right you are. I'll get on to that,' and Sam stepped briskly out of Tony's office. *The man is unbelievable!* she muttered to herself, as she went back downstairs.

'Coffee's on your desk. Well, you've still got a head on your shoulders so he can't have bitten it off,' said Jen, trying to make Sam laugh.

'He had a damned good try. Thanks, Jen, I'm going to have to keep my head down and crack on with some work stuff now.'

Jen looked at Sam's closed-up face, and decided now was not the time to talk. Leaving Sam to her work, Jen returned to her own desk, sighing. It was hard when there was nothing to do but wait.

Sam brought her marketing plan up on screen, pushing thoughts of Tony's monologue to one side. How could she make best use of Melissa? Maybe she'd like to make some short videos about the series, or perhaps even read one of the books: *Storytime with Melissa.* No, perhaps that was too much of a stretch. But some little snippets about *Granny Fi* might be fun. The videos could go on the Little Bear website, or a social media channel, if only there was one.

'Jen, who manages the website? I'm just thinking about getting some videos to upload.'

Jen gave her the name, and Sam pinged a message off. She was surprised to get a quick answer, and a positive one. Now all she needed to do was to get Melissa on board.

DS Balinski looked at the letter signed by Frank McManners and sighed. It would be easy to jump to the conclusion that Brendan had murdered his brother, but under questioning Brendan had vehemently denied it. Balinski had got access to Frank's post-mortem and inquest, and he read through them thoroughly. Clearly, Frank McManners was not in good health. He had a weak heart, and any stress or sudden shock could have been fatal. Frank knew that, but did his brother know, as Frank claimed in his letter?

He closed the files, and sat looking at the blank screen, thinking. *Brendan put Frank under a lot of pressure, according to Frank's letter. And perhaps Brendan also threatened him? Was it enough to give Frank a heart attack? Difficult to prove that Brendan had used any knowledge of Frank's dodgy heart to get him out of the way.*

'Penny for them.'

'What?' Balinski turned to see DC Chaudhury looking at him. 'Oh, I was just thinking about McManners and who he might have murdered. What did you make of the interview with him?'

'Wouldn't trust him. He's one of those people who believe they are always right, and that he doesn't have to follow the same rules as the rest of us. He's a bully. Maybe even a narcissist.'

'Hmm. I'd already worked that out, of course. We're going to have to let him go—for now, at least, but we'll keep a close eye on him.'

'Right-oh, guv. What about Price?'

'She won't be released. We'll have to put her under medical supervision.'

'Did she say anything useful?'

'Not really. Just more of what you've already heard: Brendan's a murderer because he killed his brother, and that he has to pay for what he's done. Apart from some bullying behaviour, she's said nothing that gives us reason to arrest McManners for murder, either of his brother or of his aunt. There's simply no evidence to charge him with.'

'Sounds as though Frank's death has made her mentally unstable.'

'Yeah, that'll all be checked out of course. Her medical records will be reviewed, and there'll be an assessment of her current mental state.'

'I almost feel sorry for her.'

'Hmm. I'll wait until we know more before wasting my sympathy. But now, we need to get the paperwork sorted for Brendan McManners' release.'

Chapter Ten

Inspector Keld could feel his shoulders relaxing the closer he got to Cumbria. Leaving the county of his birth always made him uneasy, as his shoulders would be the first to testify. Now he'd turned off the motorway and was driving through a quieter area of his beloved Cumbria he opened the car window to breathe in the sharp, cold air. It was raining. It was January after all, but the rain was a small price to pay for breathing fresh air.

Not that he'd have much time to get outdoors. As he approached Upper Braithwaite the questions he'd been puzzling over came back to him. The last time he'd gone inside Kaye Butterworth's house he'd felt there was something not quite right about it.

Slowing down as he approached the lane to Kaye's property, he glimpsed Nate Braithwaite in the front window of his house.

Nate opened the door to Keld's knock, holding on to Gustav's collar.

'Still trying to make a run for it, is he?' asked Keld as he bent to scratch the top of Gustav's head. Gustav wagged his agreement.

'He seems a bit more settled, but I still wouldn't trust him to make a dash back to Kaye's. How's it all going?'

'Not sure. I'm going back to the cottage now. There's something not quite right about the place but I can't put my finger on it. Perhaps you'd come with me. It would be good to have a fresh pair of eyes.'

'No problem. I'll just put Gustav inside and I'll be with you.'

Keld walked on to Kaye's cottage, which still had the police 'do not cross' plastic across the gate. He stepped over the low wall, took out a key and opened the door. Nate joined him, and they went through to the sitting room. Nate looked around carefully, a sudden shiver running down his spine as he looked at the pool of blood, now dried, near the hearthstone.

'You all right, lad?' asked Keld. 'You found her. Must bring it back for you. Is there anything different about this room, do you think?'

'No, apart from the obvious: her body's gone, even if the blood is still there. I didn't come in here very often but I can't see that anything's out of place.'

'Let's go through to the back room then.'

Keld led the way into the room Kaye used for her drawings.

'That's odd,' said Nate immediately. 'She was showing me the drawings she was working on for the latest book. She wasn't very happy with them and wanted to know what I thought. But they're not here. She might have sent them off to the publisher though.'

Keld opened the long drawers Kaye used for storing her illustrations.

'Anything here?'

'That's weird. The last time I saw those drawers open they were stuffed full of her artwork. But they're empty.'

'I see. We'd better check the rest of the house.'

'I've never gone upstairs,' said Nate, 'so I wouldn't know if anything has changed.'

'No, but you might know if there are any drawings upstairs that should be down here.'

'True. I'll follow you up.'

The two men looked into the two small bedrooms, each neatly furnished, but lacking any artwork other than framed pictures on the wall. Similarly, the bathroom yielded nothing either.

'Nothing. Where can it all be? I mean, there was a lot of paper, and some drawings were mounted on card.'

'Would they be valuable?' asked Keld.

'Her work would have a value, and quite a high one with the right buyer. But I can't see someone murdering Kaye to get her original drawings. I mean, we're not talking original Beatrix Potter,' said Nate.

'I agree. You've not noticed anyone hanging around, or going into the property?'

'I know the police have been around, but I haven't noticed anyone else. Presumably someone's secured the back door where I had to break the glass? And the house is locked now?'

'Yes, that's all sorted. We wouldn't want anyone coming in and contaminating things. Can you think of any reason why these drawings have disappeared?'

'No. I can't think why anyone would take them, especially when the house is still taped off. If someone did go in, they'd be doing it knowing they shouldn't be there.' There was a pause. 'I suppose, well, it might be worth asking Sam Holliday.'

'Good point. I've already mentioned I might need her to come back here. Anything else occur to you?'

'No, not at the moment.'

'I need to get back to the station.'

Nate took the hint, and said a quick goodbye. He felt better for being back in his own home. The brief mention of Sam Holliday gave him pause. He was surprised at how much he wanted to see her again, but there was no guarantee that would happen without a bit of a plan. A plan that didn't come across as an obvious ploy. it had been a while since he'd travelled south. And he had an open invitation to stay with friends there. He quickly checked their address, and looked it up on Google Maps. Yes, it would be good to see them … and he'd be close enough to Lower Rushford to meet up with Sam. If she wanted to.

The day had not started well for Sam, but as she left the office that evening, she felt she'd made some progress. Melissa had been delighted with the video suggestion, and even Tony had given her proposal a curt 'just do it'. She had no idea whether anyone should approve her marketing plan in Brendan's absence, but in the meantime she'd 'just do it,' as Tony put it.

As she prepared her supper, the phone buzzed and Keld's name and number appeared on the screen.

'Sam here,' she answered.

'Keld. I'm in Cumbria. I went back to the cottage today, with Nate Braithwaite. He noticed that a lot of drawings that should have been in the back room were missing. Did you see them when you visited her?'

'Good evening, Inspector.' Keld cleared his throat and mumbled something that might have been a 'good evening'.

'Yes,' continued Sam. 'Kaye took me through to her back room where she said she liked to work. There were drawings on her desk, and in the drawers she opened. Has much has gone? And why would anyone do that?'

'There's nothing in that back room, and we couldn't see anything in any of the other rooms. I'm struggling to see the art as a motive for murder though.'

'What if it was a burglar, and Kaye disturbed them?

'Possible, of course, but would her drawings have a high enough value to be worth stealing, let alone worth committing murder?'

'She was very well known, but yes, I take your point. None of it would be in the millions, maybe not even the hundreds of thousands.'

'Anything you can think of, anything you've heard while you've been working at the publisher's?' asked Keld.

'Let me think.' Sam paused, and Keld remained silent. 'Well, there's all the mystery about the payment for the printing of the latest book, and storing the copies in Brendan's garage but it looks as though that was a ruse to avoid a takeover bid. But I don't see how that would get Kaye murdered. I mean, she was probably against a takeover but even so … And she was against changing the style of the drawings so they'd appeal more to other countries. Like China.'

'Tell me more.'

Sam quickly explained about Brendan's email to Mr Cheung, and the sample drawings that looked as though they were for the Chinese market.

'He—Brendan—was definitely looking to get some kind of deal with Cheung. And if Kaye wouldn't agree, perhaps Brendan or Cheung got nasty? We know Brendan visited Kaye the night she died.'

'Hmm. Interesting. McManners will have been questioned by now, but he may still be at the police station. I'll get Balinski to explore the Cheung angle with him. We need some answers.'

'Do you need me to come up to Cumbria this weekend?'

'Not sure yet. Probably not, but I'll let you know. Goodnight.'

Sam stood for a moment looking at her screen showing the

disconnected call. He really was lacking in social niceties, but perhaps they weren't important for solving crimes, Sam thought. Could Kaye really have been murdered because she dug her heels in once too often?

Keld put down his phone. The call with Sam Holliday had been useful and straightforward. Would his next call, to DS Balinski, be as helpful? Clearly, Balinski's toes felt trodden on but he had—eventually—agreed to ask Brendan some further questions on Keld's behalf.

'You're lucky, though. I was just about to let him go,' said Balinski.

'Best step on it, then. And phone me immediately you finish with him.' Balinski grunted—Keld hoped it was in agreement—and ended the call.

Keld drummed his fingers on his desk as he waited, answering the phone at the first ring.

'Well, that was interesting.'

'Explain.'

'McManners claims that he was exploring ways to expand his publishing business by partnering with a publisher in China. The Chinese were keen on the kids' stories with that Granny Fi character, but they wouldn't accept the illustrations as they stood. Kaye wasn't interested in sales outside the UK, and certainly didn't want to make any changes to her way of drawing. So McManners got a new illustrator to re-work them. He didn't tell Kaye about it, or that he was actively pursuing a publishing deal in China.'

'What was he doing in Upper Braithwaite that night? When I interviewed him, he said he was worried about the threats—the drawings with 'murderer' written on them that were left at his office, and that he wanted to make sure Kaye hadn't received anything similar. She hadn't, according to McManners, and that seems likely as we know now that those threats were made by Enid Price and were directed only at McManners.'

'When I pressed him,' continued Balinski, 'McManners said that the company he was dealing with in China were getting impatient, and they'd threatened to speak to Kaye directly to get her approval. Brendan was uneasy about that. He knew they were more than capable of sending a delegation to her cottage. He decided to visit her in person to try to persuade her to accept an offer from China. Subject to the Chinese approving the illustrations, the deal was in the bag according to McManners. The only sticking point was Kaye. There was a lot of money involved in this contract, apparently. I'd no idea kids' books could be so lucrative. No wonder he wanted his aunt's approval.'

'And did the Chinese speak to Kaye direct?'

'He doesn't know. He doesn't think so.'

'How was he going to get the contract through without Kaye's buy-in? Ah, yes, I see. He's set up another company—Big Bear—with himself, and the two directors, Clive Frobisher and Tony Pearson. The Chinese agreement would be with Big Bear, but it would be easier if he didn't have to go down that route.'

'I wasn't aware of a second company,' said Balinski. 'Why wasn't I informed?'

'Sam Holliday told me. She was looking into an invoice for the printing of the books that were in McManners garage, and she found there was a second company that was used to pay the printer's bill. None of that's illegal, of course,' said Keld.

'Hmm. It may not be relevant to the case but it does say something about the way McManners operates.' After a pause, Balinski asked 'Do we have names for the Chinese company, and the people McManners are dealing with?'

'I've got the details. I'll run a check on them and I'll let you know what I find.'

'Good.'

Keld sat back in his chair, tapping his pen against his teeth. He was starting to get a better picture of what was going on at Little or Big Bear, but who had killed Kaye Butterworth? High on his list was Brendan McManners. No one else had been seen in Upper Braithwaite. It was such a quiet backwater that it wasn't very surprising someone had slipped in and put an end to Kaye Butterworth's life without being seen. Was it pre-meditated, or did something go wrong?

Keld went in search of a cup of tea. It would, as always, help him think through the possibilities.

Chapter Eleven

Thursday, January 27th

Sam flapped her hand in the direction of her phone, trying to turn off her alarm with minimal effort. It had not been a restful night as her dreams had repeatedly woken her up with a start. She couldn't remember them now, but she was left feeling uneasy and uncertain. The only thing she felt sure about was that she'd much prefer to stay under her duvet. But Brendan would probably be back in the office today, and she needed to be there with her marketing plan, just in case he'd remembered tomorrow's deadline.

Once out of bed, autopilot took over and she was soon out of the house and on the now familiar walk through Lower Rushford, heading for work. Spinning the revolving door to enter the offices, she tried to make her 'Hi Debbie' as bright as possible—if only to make herself feel more cheerful.

'Brendan's back. And he's not happy. I'd keep your head down if I were you,' said Debbie looking worried.

'OK, I'll try. You OK?'

'Yep, you?'

'Could be better. Here goes …'

She printed a couple of copies of her marketing plan in preparation for meeting with Brendan, and then started to think about the videos with Melissa. She wanted to include a range of the *Granny Fi* stories, and some of Kaye's artwork, so she headed downstairs to the design office.

She called out a bright 'hi' to someone with their back to her. 'Oh, hello, I didn't realise it was you, Jason. Sorry to disturb you.'

'Hi, Sam. No problem. I'm a bit engrossed in the layouts for this new book so I didn't hear you come in. Can I help you with something?'

'I'm looking for some material I could use in a video about the *Granny Fi* series, ideally from a range of the stories. And also some copies of the printed books,' said Sam.

'Stacey will have copies of all the books in her office. All the artwork's been scanned in on my computer. Kaye was old school, and drew on paper but it's been scanned in case it gets damaged.'

'Good point,' said Sam, deciding not to share the news that Kaye's originals had disappeared.

'Here, why don't you have a scroll through and let me know if there's anything you'd like to use?' suggested Jason.

'Great, thanks. I'll be as quick as I can.' Sam settled into Jason's chair and scrolled through the drawings. Once again, she was drawn in by the details, and the touches of humour. Kaye had certainly had talent.

Suddenly, the images changed from artwork to photos, mostly of publicity events for the *Granny Fi* series. As she skimmed through, the appearance of one young woman in many of the photos made Sam curious.

'Who's this, next to Brendan? She's in a lot of these photos.'

'Oh,' said Jason, looking over Sam's shoulder. 'That's Anoushka. She was the Marketing Manager before you. She put on some great events, and then all of a sudden, she was gone. Never did find out why.'

'I'd heard that too. Oh well, that doesn't matter. It's the drawings I need, and there are some lovely ones here. I've made a list of the ones I might use. Could you send me copies? I just need them for reference for now so they don't need to be best quality files.'

'Great, I'll get them over to you later today, OK?'

Sam had just sat down at her desk when Jen appeared.

'Hi, Sam. How's it going?'

'OK. How about you?'

'All right, although I've seen Brendan which didn't really make my day.'

'I can imagine. How is our Gordon No Manners?' asked Sam.

'As delightful as ever. Moaning that Enid wasn't in yet,' Jen grinned. 'He wants the marketing plan. I said you'd take it up to him as soon as you got in.'

'Ha, I'm ahead of him. Not only have I got it a day earlier than his deadline, but I've even printed off a copy for him!'

'I think that calls for coffee at Gino's later?' asked Jen.

'To celebrate or commiserate. I'm not sure which it'll be. But yes, that would be good.'

Without Enid as gatekeeper, Sam went straight through the office to find Brendan's office door shut. Taking a deep breath, she knocked firmly, going in as she heard Brendan's brusque 'Enter.'

'Good morning, Brendan. I'm so very sorry to hear about Kaye.' She didn't know whether to mention Enid, or the fire.

'What? Oh yes, thanks … er, Jan.' Sam didn't bother to correct him. There was a pause, then Brendan suddenly looked up at her. 'Weren't you supposed to meet Kaye?'

'Yes. I spent an afternoon with her, talking about her illustrations. She was very interesting.'

'Hmm. Well, that's all finished now. We've just got to make what we can from the books we have. Where's the marketing plan?'

'Here. Do you want me to talk you through it? Melissa was keen to be involved, so I've suggested we work together to create some short videos about the books. We can put them on the website, and link to the books.'

'That'll keep her busy, if nothing else. Not going to cost much, is it? We haven't got Hollywood budgets, you know.'

'No, I can set it up myself. About the plan—bear in mind when you read it that I couldn't get the sales data I wanted. Clive was going to get me access, but with everything else I think it's slipped his mind and I didn't want to pester him.'

'You saw the sales graph in the meeting with Melissa. Sales have flat-lined, and unless your marketing plan is any good, sales will take a complete nose dive.'

'It will take more than marketing. Booksellers need stock, and the stories have to appeal to our customers,' said Sam, trying to keep her tone neutral.

Brendan shot her a sharp look at the mention of stock but didn't comment.

'OK then, I'll leave you to look through the rest of the plan,' said Sam.

'Good. Oh, and give me back the plan your predecessor wrote. I'll know if you've just copied it.'

'I'll bring it up to you.'

Gordon No Manners, Sam thought as she turned away to leave the office. *The arrogance of the man! And all he can think of is what Kaye's death means for sales. He's as bad as Melissa.*

Back at her desk, she picked up her predecessor's marketing plan and flicked through it. She certainly hadn't copied the ideas intentionally, but some ideas were simply common sense and those *were* in her plan. Turning to the last page she read a scribbled note that she hadn't noticed before.

Great work. Dinner tonight to celebrate? B xx

What did that mean? 'B' could only mean Brendan, couldn't it? Another clandestine relationship? A bit unethical, but not criminal. Sam remembered that the previous manager, Anoushka, had left suddenly. The end of the relationship, or perhaps she hadn't wanted a relationship with Brendan? Sam would probably never know. She went back to Brendan's office and gave him Anoushka's plan. A grunt was the only thanks.

Sam decided to call Melissa to discuss the videos in more detail.

'Melissa Bingley,' snapped a voice that couldn't belong to anyone else.

'This is Sam Holliday, from Little Bear.'

'Oh yes, the marketing woman. What's the plan with these videos you want to do?'

'That's what I wanted to talk to you about.' Sam outlined her thoughts, leaving plenty of opportunity for Melissa to add her ideas, and to amend Sam's. *Definitely a control freak*, thought Sam.

'Well, that all seems very good. I'm sure people will love seeing me. Can't think why we haven't done this before.'

'I've no idea. But yes, there should be a lot of interest, which hopefully will mean more sales. Now, when can you come in for filming?'

'I'm back in Manchester now, and I'll need to see my hairdresser and beautician.'

'I didn't realise you were in Manchester. I'd assumed you were local.'

'No, I stay at Brendan's when I'm attending meetings but otherwise I'm here. How about Monday? I can't get hold of Brendan so I'll have to sort out accommodation. I can't get hold of that miserable secretary of his either. Wait—you could book me in somewhere. Somewhere suitable, I mean. After all the palaver with the nail varnish, I think I deserve a particularly good hotel,' said Melissa, placing a clear emphasis on 'good'.

'Of course, Melissa. I'll book you in to Lower Rushford's very best,' Sam replied, thinking *Poor Enid! She had to put up with this every time Melissa came to the office.*

'Right, Monday at 10 at the office then. I'll send you some photos of what I'm thinking of wearing. I want to make sure it will look good on camera.'

'Great, and I'll confirm your hotel booking. Look forward to working with you.' *Like hell,* thought Sam, as Melissa ended the call.

'Jen,' Sam called. 'I'm pretty sure I'm ready for that coffee now.'

The coffee smelt just as good as Sam remembered it. The waiter remembered them from their lunch which felt like many months ago to them. Wrapping their hands around the steaming cups of coffee, Jen asked Sam how she'd got on with Brendan. Sam explained, and told her about the previous marketing plan with its invitation for dinner.

'Oh, I'd forgotten about that. Yes, Brendan seemed quite interested in Anoushka—well, for Brendan. I mean, he always remembered her name.'

'Sounds as though I won't be getting any invites for a dinner date then,' commented Sam. 'He still can't remember mine.'

'Disappointed?' grinned Jen.

'Devastated,' replied Sam trying to keep a straight face.

'So how do things stand now?' Jen asked.

Sam thought for a moment. She couldn't tell her about Enid and the fire. Brendan hadn't referred to either, but perhaps that was to be expected as both involved things he wouldn't want anyone to know about. Not to mention his arrest.

'I've told Inspector Keld about the other company, but he says that's not part of the investigation. I haven't heard anything more about Kaye. There have been some other things happening but I have a feeling we'll be briefed on those so I'd better not say anything.'

'OK. Wonder if anyone took the bait with the drawings,' wondered Jen.

'Hmm,' said Sam, nibbling the amoretto biscuit that came with her coffee.

Once again, Sam found herself sitting at a desk with her Little Bear colleagues, at the request of DS Balinski. Balinski shuffled some papers, cleared his throat, and looked up to meet the twenty or so expectant faces.

Chapter Eleven

'I'm here to give you an update. You'll no doubt be relieved to hear that we have arrested the perpetrator of the malicious threats.'

There was a collective intake of breath from around the table, and a few people exclaimed.

'Enid Price has been arrested and charged with making malicious threats against Brendan McManners, and also for arson and attempted murder.'

The room exploded with cries of disbelief and shock.

'I can assure you that this is true, and that Enid Price has made a confession to this effect. There is nothing more I can tell you at this stage.'

'Do you mean Enid Price is charged with Kaye Butterworth's murder?' asked Jason Lee. There was incredulity in his voice, which reflected the reaction around the table.

'We don't believe so. The Butterworth case is in the hands of Inspector Keld, in Cumbria, as that is where the crime was committed. He is, of course, working closely with myself and DC Chaudhury.'

'So who did she try to murder? And what's this about arson?' followed up Jason.

'I'm unable to give any further details at this time. This is an ongoing investigation, and all I can do at the moment is assure you that there are unlikely to be any further malicious threats. We are confident we have arrested the right person, and she has admitted she made the threats.'

'But why did she do it?' asked another person.

'Again, I'm not at liberty to tell you more. Your directors are going to speak to you, so please remain here until they have done so.' Collecting together his sheets of paper, Balinski left the room, just as Tony Pearson and Clive Frobisher entered.

'Well,' opened Tony, shuffling on his chair. 'You know the latest. No doubt there will be more media attention. I do not want *anyone* appearing in the press so be very careful how you behave,' he said with a meaningful look in Sam's direction.

'Brendan will be without a secretary for the time being. He is back in the office today, and he'll expect to find you working as usual. Questions?' He looked around the table, but most people looked too shocked to want to speak.

'Right, back to it then,' said Clive, almost clapping his hands together to chivvy everyone along.

It's almost as though they're enjoying themselves, thought Sam.

'Get in here,' snapped Brendan, as he saw Clive and Tony standing in his outer office. 'There's a lot to talk about.'

'We've just spoken to the troops. They all seemed a bit dismayed but we made it clear that it's business as usual,' reported Tony.

'Too right,' said Brendan. 'Keep their noses to the grindstone, and that'll keep them out of our business. Now then, I've had Harvey's on the phone. They've reviewed latest sales, and heard the news. They've got cold feet and there will be no takeover offer for the foreseeable. That's one problem out of the way for now.'

'Good. What about Cheung?' asked Clive.

'Just had a call with him. He knows Kaye's dead but that doesn't affect our deal with them as his people like the work I sent them from the new illustrator. He's keen to move to the next stage, and his legal people have drawn up a draft contract. We'll need to get your legal firm, Clive, to advise us on that. We should be able to approve it at the next Big Bear Board meeting, later this month, if the contract is straightforward.'

'The legal people are expecting the paperwork so we'll get their view in a couple of days,' said Clive.

'Good. We've just got to hold steady and get through this mess. At least Enid won't be causing any more trouble, and we'll just have to ride out the media interest in Kaye's murder. The police aren't interested in the books in my garage. The only crime was Enid's arson attempt. I've got to sort out the insurance and get my garage repaired, which is a pain. Other than that, there'll be the coroner's court to give a verdict on Kaye's death, and eventually the funeral, which will be a private, family affair. What we don't need right now is people sticking their noses in where it's not needed.'

'You're thinking about that marketing woman?' asked Tony.

'Exactly, yes, Pam, Fran, whatever her name is.'

'She's working on some videos with Melissa. Should keep both of them out of our hair for a bit,' said Tony. 'Balinski told me that Jason Lee asked a few questions about Enid being charged with attempted murder and arson, but he wasn't able to give Jason any details.'

'Make sure you keep a lid on all that. We don't want any rumours getting out. Right, I think we're done. I'll let you know when I get the draft contract.'

Sam threw her bag onto the sofa, and went through to the kitchen to make some tea. It had been a long day, but at least it was nearly the weekend. What she needed, she thought, was something to take her mind of everything that had happened. Something to look forward to. Walking was her usual antidote, and she suddenly remembered the walking group she'd seen on the Lower Rushford website. Scrolling through on her phone she found a reply to her enquiry, with links to information for the walk on Saturday. It looked a good one. Just what she needed.

Remembering she hadn't yet replied to Nate's kind email, she wrote a short, friendly reply. Drinking her tea, and starting to prepare her meal, her phone pinged with Nate's reply.

> Some friends have invited me to stay with them for the weekend, so I'm travelling down to Cirencester tomorrow. Any chance you're free Sunday lunch time to meet for a drink, or lunch? Would be good to see you.

Sam hesitated. It sounded very like a date, and Sam had decided to steer clear of dates after leaving Jack. But it would be good to see Nate, she thought, and, if necessary, she could always make it clear that she wanted friendship and nothing more. So why not say yes? She needed to take her mind off the last few days but if she did need to talk about what had happened, she knew Nate was a good listener. She replied, confirming, and asked him to ask his friends to suggest a pub between Cirencester and Lower Rushford. She texted her mum to say she was fine, and to let her know she had some nice things lined up for the weekend. That would stop Elaine worrying.

Chapter Twelve

Friday, January 28th

It was a cold and miserable January morning, and Sam checked the forecast for the weekend. It looked as though Saturday would be brighter, and Sunday looked promising too, before returning to rain for the rest of the week.

Sam got ready for work with a heavy heart. It was difficult to remember how excited she'd felt less than two weeks ago about starting her new job. She'd deflected Brendan's threat to fire her by producing the marketing plan, but although she needed the income she wasn't at all sure she wanted to continue with Little Bear. But any thoughts about a move would have to wait.

The atmosphere was quiet at work, almost eerily so. It felt as though people were reluctant to talk beyond a noncommittal 'hi'. Sam gave a quick wave to Jen and then settled at her desk. Melissa had emailed with some photos to finalise her clothes for the videos, and Sam remembered to book a local hotel for her. She worked on the video ideas, storyboarding the content for each one, keeping it short and hopefully fun for viewers. It was difficult to be lighthearted, but Sam focused on her work and felt she'd made some progress. She sorted out a room for filming, and spoke to her colleagues in design and editorial to get their input. She was ready for Monday's filming, although she doubted she would ever feel ready for Melissa.

Chapter Thirteen

Saturday, January 29th

Sam packed her waterproofs, a few snacks, and a drink into her backpack. No need for maps, as someone else was leading the walk, and they were stopping at a pub to eat. She simply needed to put one foot in front of the other (without tripping over a stone this time), and enjoy the walk. She laced up her walking boots and shrugged the pack onto her shoulders.

Stepping out into weak sunshine, Sam headed towards the town car park to meet the rest of the group. It wasn't hard to spot them. Everyone had a small backpack and wore walking boots. She was relieved to see that there were no more than eight in the group which would make it easier to keep moving, even over stiles, and to have a chance to talk to everyone.

'Hi, I'm Sam, I emailed to say I'd like to join the walk today.' She looked around the group, waiting for the organiser to identify themselves.

'Hi Sam, I'm Lizzie Fielding—yeah, I know, I had to be an outdoorsy type with that surname!' Lizzie held out her hand to

Sam. 'Oh sorry, are you OK with shaking hands now? Or shall we elbow bump?'

'Don't worry, a handshake is fine. It does still feel a bit strange though, doesn't it. And that's a great surname, by the way! I'm really glad to join the walk today.'

'Let me introduce you to the rest of the group .... Mike and Rachel, Ruby and Doug, Lorraine, Flis, and Anoushka.'

Sam was exchanging a quick 'hi' with each person as they were introduced. Hearing 'Anoushka,' Sam gave a start. Looking more closely at the person introduced as Anoushka she realised that this was her predecessor at Little Bear, even if she did look rather different in a woolly hat.

'Do I know you?' asked Anoushka, frowning as Sam stared at her just a little too long.

'No, sorry, it's just that your face looked familiar. Great to meet you,' said Sam.

Any further conversation was cut short by Lizzie quickly explaining the route they'd take on the walk, and that if everyone was ready, they could set off. Sam fell into step with Lorraine, chatting as the group headed away from the car park to pick up a footpath that led away from the town. As they walked, everyone made an effort to speak to Sam as the newest member of the group. Eventually, she found herself walking with Anoushka.

'It's great having a weekend walking group,' Sam said. 'I only moved here recently, and I'm working all week. I'm always desperate to get outdoors by the time Saturday comes round. I've never walked in this area.'

'Yes, I like to get out and away from the desk too, especially at this time of the year. I moved here about a year ago, and it's been a good way to get to know a few people. What sort of work do you do?'

'I work in marketing,' replied Sam.

'Oh, interesting, so do I. Where do you work?' asked Anoushka.

'For the publishing company in town, Little Bear,' said Sam, avoiding looking at Anoushka as she answered.

'Really? I worked there for a time. How are you getting on?'

'Oh, what a coincidence! I've only been there for a couple of weeks but they seem nice people.'

'Even Brendan?' asked Anoushka.

Sam turned to look at her. 'Well, no, maybe not. But everyone else is fine. How did you get on with Brendan?'

'I didn't. *He* thought we got on, but he gave me the creeps. He fired me in the end.'

'What? How did he get away with that?'

'Long story. If you really want to know, I'll tell you when we stop at the pub. Otherwise you won't get a chance to talk with the others. What are you working on? *Granny Fi,* I suppose.'

Sam nodded. 'And yes, I've met the delightful Melissa.'

'And Kaye?' asked Anoushka.

'Haven't you heard? I'm sorry if this is a shock, but Kaye died.'

'What? When? I had no idea she was ill.'

'Just a few days ago. It's awful. Sorry to tell you this, but the police believe it was murder.'

'No!' Anoushka stopped abruptly, and turned to Sam. 'We really have to talk. We'll have more time over lunch. Look, I need to talk to Flis before she thinks I'm ignoring her. Why don't you join Lizzie; she always likes to talk about the route she's planned.'

'Good idea,' and Sam walked briskly to catch up with Lizzie.

Lizzie explained that she'd started the group a couple of years ago with her friends, Mike and Rachel. Meeting most weekends, unless the weather was too awful, they explored the local area, going further afield in summer.

'It's a great way to meet people, especially if you're new to the area,' said Lizzie.

'Yes, I moved here from Kidlington which isn't that far away really, but it feels very different here.'

'It's a great area for walking. Plenty of footpaths, and some options for when it gets really muddy. We're not going too far today. We'll be at the pub for around 1, and we won't have far to walk once we leave there to get back to town.'

Lizzie talked more about some of the walks she hoped to organise, and Sam shared her recent walking experience in Cumbria.

Lizzie was sympathetic about Sam's ankle, which seemed to be bearing up well on today's walk. The countryside's sepia colour scheme had a certain beauty to it: ploughed fields with earth of various shades of brown, brown tree trunks, and muddy brown paths. It wasn't everyone's idea of loveliness, but Sam enjoyed being outdoors and the feeling of movement as she passed by the naked-looking trees. Through their bare branches, Sam could see the gently rolling hills, and hoped she'd one day climb them.

The miles slipped by as Sam enjoyed the landscape and the friendly conversation of the group. Lizzie announced they would reach the pub in about half an hour, and Sam realised how hungry she felt, despite nibbling on some nuts and fruit along the way.

The pub, with a roaring open fire, was a welcome sight to the walkers. Food and drinks ordered, they found a large table they could all sit round. Anoushka sat next to Sam, and immediately asked her to tell her more about Kaye. Sam told her as much as she could, and Anoushka listened in growing disbelief.

'It must be really difficult working there at the moment,' she commented.

'Yes, it's a very sombre atmosphere, and—oh, I haven't told you about Enid Price.'

'Brendan's secretary?' asked Anoushka.

'Former secretary now, I should think.'

'What? But she was devoted to the company, especially to Frank McManners. He died just before I left. It was tragic, especially for Enid.'

'I think Frank's death may have pushed her too far. She blamed Brendan for what happened,' explained Sam.

'Ah, I see.' Anoushka looked thoughtful, before saying 'I know Brendan wanted to expand into China. He asked me to come up with a marketing plan for that. But I don't think all the Board were in agreement. Frank made it very clear he wasn't in favour, and I'm fairly sure Kaye wouldn't have wanted to re-draw her illustrations. She would have hated that.'

'You're right about Kaye. What about Melissa? Did she know about the China plan?'

'She did—and she was all for it. She was really angry about Kaye not supporting it, and said she'd try to win her round. No chance of that now, though.'

'So why was Melissa raging about the current *Granny Fi* sales if she knew about this China deal?'

'Nothing was certain. She probably wanted to have her cake and eat it, knowing Melissa,' said Anoushka.

'Not talking work, are you?' called Lizzie from the other end of the table. 'It's a walking day, not a working day!' she said, half-jokingly.

'Anoushka worked for the company I've now joined. But you're right, let's not talk about work now,' said Sam.

Anoushka got out her phone. 'If you'd like to talk more, I can give you my mobile number?'

'Thanks, that would be great,' replied Sam. Numbers exchanged, they both made a point of talking to the rest of the group as they waited for their food to arrive.

It didn't take long to walk from the pub to the original meeting point. Sam told Lizzie how much she'd enjoyed walking with the group, and promised to join another walk soon.

'That's great,' said Lizzie. 'It would be good to have you as part of the group. The next one will be in a couple of weeks. I haven't quite decided where it will be yet. I tend to keep an eye on the weather, and decide on a route closer to the date. The details will be on the website, but you've got my contact details if you've got any questions.'

'Thanks, Lizzie,' said Sam. Waving, she walked briskly back home, ready for a hot shower before curling up on the sofa with her book.

Although the sofa was comfortable, and the book was a good one, for some reason Sam couldn't settle. Something was niggling her. Someone had said something to her that made her feel uneasy. What was it? She was still puzzling over it as she headed for bed, but after all the fresh air and exercise sleep soon overcame her.

Chapter Fourteen

Sunday, January 30th

Sam's morning was a leisurely one until she realised that she needed to leave soon to meet Nate for lunch. Scrabbling through her wardrobe, she wondered what to wear. Jeans? Too casual: she should make some effort. Dress? No, that was trying too hard. In the end she settled for her favourite black velvety leggings, a long colourful top and a silky scarf. It really did feel like getting ready for a date, and she had to remind herself it was nothing more than lunch with a friend. And there was no reason why she shouldn't wear something nice—the effort was for her, not Nate, she told herself.

She'd already checked the route to the pub, and it was an easy drive. Pushing open the door, she was met with a blast of warm air and chatter. Looking around she soon saw Nate and waved. He got up and gave her a quick hug and a kiss on the cheek, asking her how she was getting on. It was, Sam decided, good to see him again, and she felt comfortable with his friendly greeting.

As they settled down to eat their lunch of roast beef and Yorkshire puddings, Nate told her that there was no further news about Kaye. 'The house is locked up, of course, and I've still got Gustav.'

'How is he?' Sam asked.

'He's doing quite well. I've got a couple of photos on my phone.'

As they were looking at the photos a loud voice made them both jump

'Ooh look, isn't this cosy? Didn't take you long, did it, Sam Holliday?'

Sam looked up, dismayed to see Jack's face and his gleeful expression.

'Who's the new lover-boy then—aren't you going to introduce us?'

'No. No, I'm not,' said Sam.

'Oh dear, still grumpy. Can't be getting enough …'

Sam cut in with 'Go away, Jack. What I do, and who I'm with, is nothing to do with you.' She wrapped her hands around her glass so Jack couldn't see them shaking.

'I wish you joy with her, mate. She's a miserable cow, as you may already know.'

Without waiting for any reaction or response, Jack sauntered off, leaving Sam and Nate feeling very embarrassed.

'You don't need to explain,' said Nate.

'Thanks for saying that,' said Sam. 'I'm really embarrassed to admit that I lived with that idiot for five years before I came to my senses. I left him last year, and moved away to start a new job. I had no idea he'd be here today. It must just be some horrible coincidence.'

Nate nodded to indicate a group that was behind Sam. 'He's with some mates. Judging by all the Lycra, he's part of a cycling group,' said Nate.

'Yes, he used to go off cycling when I lived with him. A coincidence then. For one moment, I thought he was stalking me,' said Sam, her voice sounding shaky.

'You've had a difficult time,' said Nate.

'Yes. He was really nice at first, and we had some good times, until he decided I couldn't do anything right. He really undermined my confidence. I ended up seeing a counsellor. My manager set that up for me, and she, the counsellor I mean, helped me realise what was happening. Eventually I got up the courage to leave.'

'That was brave,' Nate said.

Glancing up at him, she saw that he wasn't laughing at her as she feared. In his face there was nothing but concern and understanding.

'Let's talk about something else, shall we?' Sam suggested. 'How's your book coming on?' Back on safe ground, conversation flowed until Nate noticed it was now dark, and late into the afternoon.

'You'll need to get home,' he said. 'And I'd better get back to my friends' place.'

'Are you driving back to Cumbria tonight?' asked Sam.

'No, tomorrow. Look, I've really enjoyed today, and I hope they'll be another chance to meet up.'

Sam hesitated. 'Yes,' she said slowly. 'Yes, I'd like that.'

'Great, stay in touch, and hopefully we can work something out.' He got up to put on his coat, and turned to hug Sam goodbye. She found she really rather enjoyed Nate's hugs. And she really didn't care what Jack made of it.

Chapter Fifteen

Monday, January 31st

Inspector Keld drummed his fingers on his desktop. It had been a frustrating few days, waiting for the detailed autopsy report. He was sure Kaye's death was not accidental, but he needed confirmation. He was no further forward with finding out who had caused her death.

He picked up his phone, found the contact he wanted, and waited impatiently for Ben Anderson, the pathologist, to pick up the call.

'Where's the autopsy report for Kaye Butterworth?'

'Good morning, Keld. I sent it through to you on Friday.'

'You can't have done. I've got nothing here.'

Anderson sighed. 'We've been having a few problems with the system recently. Hold on, I'll try again.'

'Humph. While you're waiting for technology to catch up, perhaps you could take me through the headlines.'

'Hmm. The cause of death was the injury to the head. Her skull was quite thin: it wouldn't have taken much to break it.'

'What do you think was used to deliver the blow?' asked Keld.

'I'd say it was most likely caused by her striking something hard, rather than anyone bludgeoning her.'

'You mean she probably fell and hit her head? A hearthstone, or table then?'

'Something of that sort, yes,' confirmed the pathologist.

'What else?'

'She'd clearly tried to break her fall. There's scrapings of hair and skin under her fingernails. They're not likely to be hers. I'd put money on someone else being with her when she fell.'

'And yet no one called the emergency services. Well, at least now we have something to work on.'

'Right. I've sent the report through again. Let me know if it still doesn't reach you.'

'Will do.' Keld ended the call, and immediately put through another one, this time to DS Balinski.

'Keld here,' he said, cutting short any attempt at small talk as Balinski picked up the phone. 'The cause of Kaye Butterworth's death is confirmed: she died as a result of the blow to her head.'

'I thought we knew that already.'

'We *suspected* that was the cause. The pathologist's report confirms it. But there's more.' Keld talked through the information he'd just heard from the pathologist. 'The question now is what caused her to fall, and does the reason for her fall amount to murder, bearing in mind the person who saw her die did not try to get help, let alone call the emergency services,' Keld explained.

'It might have been a terrible accident, and not murder after all?'

'An accident, perhaps. But whoever caused the accident left her there, knowing she was likely to die. We need to find out who the skin and hair scrapings belong to. Why did she need to grab on to this person? She must have been quite panicked to have held on enough to pull out their hair. Who was that someone? That's what I want to know.'

'Hmm. We've got a few to choose from, haven't we? McManners, Sam Holliday, the neighbour who found her.'

'Yes. I'll get DNA checks run on Nate Braithwaite. Could you organise it for Sam Holliday. In fact, I think we should check everyone working for McManners, and that includes the author. Enid Price used the author's nail varnish to write on the drawings. What was the woman's name?'

He heard Balinski turning pages in his notebook.

'Bingley. Melissa Bingley.'

'That's the one. Include her.'

'She lives in Manchester, although she does come down to Lower Rushford quite regularly. I'll deal with her if she's around, otherwise it might be easier for you to contact her?'

'Yes. Send me her details then, and I'll get on to her.' Keld put his phone down.

It was always the same when you had to check people you instinctively liked, having to suspend the disbelief that they could, after all, have committed a terrible crime. Well, it wouldn't be for the first time that he had to do something he'd take no pleasure in. He'd start with Nate Braithwaite.

'Hello.'

'Keld here.'

'What can I do …' but Keld cut him short.

'We're making progress with Kaye Butterworth's case, but I need to get your DNA. For elimination.'

'Oh, I see.' Although Nate was used to Keld's brusqueness it was still a shock to know he had to be checked in this way. 'What would you like me to do? I won't be back home until later today. I'm in the Cotswolds at the moment.'

'Can you drive straight to the station as soon as you get back here? We'll sort things out from there. Can you be there for 6?'

'I'll try my best, but it will depend on traffic,' explained Nate.

'Understood.'

Keld's next call was to Sam Holliday. He liked the young woman, and he wanted to bring her up to date as much as he could with the case, and to forewarn her of the DNA check.

'Poor Kaye,' said Sam when she heard Keld's news. 'Let's hope you can now find who was with her, and then at least we can finally know what happened. Thank you for phoning me, and of course I'll keep this to myself.'

Sensible young woman, thought Keld. He rang the last number on his list for Melissa Bingley but got no reply. He opened the file with the full autopsy report, and settled down to read it in detail.

'You want *WHAT*?'

Balinski held the phone a little further away from his ear. He had expected this type of response from Brendan McManners, and he hadn't been disappointed.

'It's for purposes of elimination, Mr McManners.'

'I did NOT murder my aunt, Sargeant. We've been through this already.'

'And this will prove that, Mr McManners.'

'Oh, I suppose I have no choice anyway,' said Brendan grumpily.

'It is a chargeable offence to refuse to assist the police with their enquiries,' advised Balinski neutrally.

'Is it indeed. Well, we can't have that. What's the drill?'

Balinski explained, and then added 'We need DNA from everyone who works for you, plus Melissa Bingley. Ms Bingley lives in Manchester, I believe?'

'Everyone? Good God! Well, if it gets the case solved, so be it. What? Melissa? Yes, she lives in Manchester, but she'll be in the office here this week.'

'Good. I can brief your staff at say, 12?'

'I'll tell them,' said Brendan.

Brendan strode to his office door, and shouted down the corridor. 'Tony, Clive! In here, now.' He didn't need to call twice.

'What's up?' asked Tony, taking in Brendan's red face.

'Police, that's what's up,' replied Brendan.

'What do they want now?'

'The DNA of everyone who works here. Even Melissa. She's going to love that. Get that marketing woman in here now. We need to manage Melissa. I can't stand the woman, but we need her.'

'DNA?' queried Clive. 'Why?'

'For purposes of elimination. I know no more than that.'

'So, the police think any of us could have murdered Kaye? That's crazy!' said Clive.

'Just do it,' snapped Brendan. 'If we don't, they'll have us up for preventing them doing their job.'

Clive's face looked several shades paler than usual. 'Right,' he said, taking off his glasses and polishing them vigorously.

'Yes, point taken,' said Tony, smoothing back his hair with nervous hands. 'Anything else?'

'The police are briefing everyone at 12. Make sure everyone's there, and get me that marketing woman!'

'You—Brendan's office, now!'

Sam jumped. She'd been concentrating on the storyboards for the upcoming videos, and hadn't heard Tony approaching her desk.

'Good morning, Tony. Yes, of course,' she said, sounding calmer than she felt. *Who the hell does he think he is?* she wondered as she walked with as much dignity as she could muster towards the stairs, and Brendan's office.

'Good morning, Brendan. You wanted to see me?'

'Yes, get in here and close the door.'

Sam's eyebrows rose a fraction at the abruptness of Brendan's tone. *Definitely Gordon No Manners today,* she thought.

'Melissa is coming in today—right?'

'Yes, we're starting work on the videos. She'll be here any minute.'

'Well, the police are going to want to see her. They'll be briefing everyone at 12—apparently, they need everyone's DNA to eliminate them from Kaye's murder. And that means everyone, even Melissa.'

'Ah,' said Sam, not letting on that she knew about the DNA tests already. 'She's not going to like that, is she.'

'You can say that again. So, you need to explain to her before the briefing, so she'll go along with it. Declining is not an option. The police have made it clear that would amount to refusing to assist them with their enquiries, or some such mumbo-jumbo.'

'I'll find a way of putting it to her then,' said Sam with a heavy heart. *As if the videos aren't stressful enough!*

'Off you go, then,' said Brendan, waving his hand at her as though she was an annoying fly.

Sam returned to her desk just as her phone starting ringing. It was Debbie at reception, announcing Melissa's arrival.

'Hello, Melissa. How are you? I hope your hotel's comfortable?'

'It'll do, I suppose. Dreadful breakfast. I need coffee.'

'Of course. I'll get one for you,' said Sam.

'Not that instant muck you have here. Someone will have to go out and get me a proper coffee.'

Sam caught Debbie's eye. There was a small grin on Debbie's face.

'No problem, I'll ask someone to go out for you. What would you like, Melissa? And Sam, what about you?' asked Debbie.

It was going to be a long day. Their coffee order noted, Sam took Melissa through to the room they would be using for filming, where the computer was set up with the storyboards. Melissa looked around the room, tutted, and took off her coat.

'I suppose it will do,' she said.

'The focus will be on you, Melissa, and we'll use a green screen so we can put images from the stories behind it, or whatever you feel is appropriate,' Sam explained.

'Well, of course. After all, these videos are about me, as the author and creator of *Granny Fi*,' snapped Melissa.

'Now, before we start, there's something Brendan asked me to tell you about.'

Melissa looked at her quizzically. 'Why isn't he telling me himself,' she asked.

'Oh, he knew I was meeting with you today, and he didn't want to waste any of your time with a separate meeting.'

'I see,' said Melissa, looking slightly less affronted.

'It concerns Kaye,' started Sam. 'The good news is that the police are getting closer to understanding what happened. But to help them with that, we've all been asked to provide some DNA ...' Melissa was looking puzzled. 'It's so we can be eliminated from their enquiries,' Sam concluded.

'And how does this affect me?' asked Melissa.

'The police will want your DNA too.' Sam felt slightly sick in anticipation of the fury that was sure to erupt.

'Mine? Why mine?' asked Melissa. The reaction was milder than Sam had feared, but she was still in the danger zone.

'I don't know. But we all have to do this.'

'They do realise who I am?' Melissa's eyes were bulging slightly with indignation. 'I'm not sure I'll agree to it.'

'It's to help them understand what happened to Kaye. Everyone's going to feel uncomfortable about giving up their DNA, but it's for Kaye.'

'Humph,' said Melissa. 'Well, I suppose if you put it like that, I might have to go along with it. I'll think about it.'

'Thank you, Melissa, I'm sure the police will appreciate your help. As would Kaye.'

Melissa gave her a puzzled look. 'Kaye's dead,' she said.

'Yes, but ... well, never mind. Let's get back to the videos, shall we? The police are coming in at 12, and I'll have to be at the briefing. I can let you know what we have to do, if don't want to be there.'

'You're not going to herd me in to any briefing as though I'm one of the resident sheep,' said Melissa.

'Of course not, Melissa. You're far too respected for that to happen. Now, the first video opens with .... '

Keld was deep in thought. The names of the people who could have been with Kaye at the time of her death—who could have caused her death—were on a neatly handwritten list in front of him. Who could have been at Kaye's cottage that evening, and why? Nate could have called in and done it, but why would he want Kaye dead? Or Sam Holliday? Was it the murderer who returned to Kaye's house to steal the drawings, and if so, why? His eye ran down the list of Little Bear's employees. He still wasn't convinced by Brendan McManners' account of his visit to Kaye. Could it have got violent? A good shove from McManners and Kaye could easily have toppled backwards.

And then there was Melissa Bingley, the author of the *Granny Fi* series. She and Kaye must have been close, given all the books they had created together. Did they actually work together, or through the staff at Little Bear? Kaye was clearly an introvert, possibly even a recluse, which made it hard to imagine her sharing her living or working space with someone else, even the author of the stories. Were the two alike, perhaps, in the way they worked? Sam Holliday would probably have formed an opinion of both people. It was worth giving her a quick call.

Some minutes later, Keld had his answer. Melissa's need to be in the limelight would have been difficult for Kaye. He couldn't see them working together in a confined space. But Melissa, as he now knew, lived in Manchester, so it would be easy enough for her to visit Kaye. Had she done so on that fateful night? And why?

Or perhaps another person in the company had travelled to Cumbria. It was a long drive, but not out of the question. There was clearly something going on with the directors at Little Bear, otherwise, why set up a separate company? Did Kaye know? Did she threaten to reveal what was happening?

Keld put down his pen, and went to make some tea. The DNA results were going to be very interesting. Someone, or some people, on his list would have a lot of explaining to do before the week was out.

Chapter Fifteen

The briefing was underway, and Sam took a moment to cast her eyes around the table. Everyone was listening to Balinski intently, and their reactions varied from shock, to anger, or to nervousness.

'And what happens to our DNA when we're eliminated from this case,' asked one of the staff. Balinski explained, reassuring them that it would not be kept unnecessarily.

'There is a list of names and appointments here,' continued Balinski, passing the information around the table. There are also details about where you need to go, and what to expect. Please be sure to keep your appointment. It will only take a few minutes out of your day, but failure to attend, without giving prior notice, could be deemed to be refusing to help the police with our enquiries, which could lead to a prison sentence.'

There were a few gasps at this, and Sam noticed that everyone made sure they had taken a copy of the information.

'Unless there are any questions, that's everything from me for now.' Balinski waited a minute, but no one said anything.

'Sam, I'd like a quick word, please, once everyone has gone back to their desks,' said Balinski. Sam felt everyone's eyes on her, and her face flushed. She hoped she didn't look guilty.

As everyone left the office, Sam could hear the buzz of their voices. She turned her attention to Balinski.

'Sam, I feel I owe you an apology,' started Balinski.

'Oh? Why,' asked Sam.

'I'm afraid I let slip that you worked here to Jack Henshaw. I shouldn't have said anything, but I thought you were still together, and I was just making conversation. It was unprofessional of me, and I'm really very sorry. I hope it won't cause any problems. He didn't seem to know where you worked, and he looked quite pleased to find out. That's what made me feel even more uncomfortable that I'd told him.'

Sam sighed. So, she'd been right, although Balinski hadn't given Jack her address. How did he find it out?

'I left him at the end of last year. I knew he wouldn't take it well so I'd already planned to move to a new area and to a new job. He turned up on my doorstep yesterday evening.'

Balinski looked shocked. 'I only let slip that you worked here. I didn't give him your home address,' he said.

'But he found it somehow, unless he was just passing as I walked back from the station.'

'It had to be coincidence,' said Balinski. 'Is everything OK?'

'I wanted to make a clean break, but he would have probably found me at some point. After all, I haven't moved that far from Kidlington. I wanted stay reasonably close to my family and friends. Don't worry, I'll deal with him,' said Sam.

'I'm really sorry, Sam,' said Balinski.

Sam gave him a weak smile, and said 'I think I've left Melissa for long enough. I'd better get back to her.'

'She'll need to provide her DNA too,' said Balinski. 'Either here, or when she gets back to Manchester. Inspector Keld will contact her if she doesn't do it before she leaves Lower Rushford.'

'I'll remind her, but she's not going to like it,' said Sam.

'She'll like being arrested for preventing the police from doing their work even less,' said Balinski, as Sam left the room.

Sam closed her front door behind her, threw her bag on the sofa, and gave a heavy sigh. What a day! She was grateful to come home to a quiet house, and to be on her own. Pandering to Melissa's considerable ego was exhausting, and Sam knew she'd struggle to say a pleasant word to anyone this evening. Still, Melissa's sense of her own importance had meant she'd stayed focused on the filming, wanting everything she did to be perfect. Of course, feedback on anything that was less than perfect had to be handled very carefully, but Sam had quickly found a way to handle Melissa and her predictably outrageous behaviour. There were just a few things to finish tomorrow, and then Melissa could go back to Manchester, once she'd complied with the DNA testing, of course.

Peeling vegetables for her supper, Sam's mind turned to Kaye. She admired Kaye's talent, and her determination that Granny Fi should not be tampered with, even if it did mean losing out financially. Melissa, of course, would have no such scruples. *Melissa was really angry with Kaye, and said she'd try to win her round. Where did that come from?* Sam paused, peeler in mid-air. Anoushka! Yes, that was the comment she was trying to recall the other evening. *Melissa was going to try to win Kaye round.* Did she try? What did she do? Perhaps she could sound Melissa out tomorrow. Keld would no doubt appreciate whatever she found out.

'Don't waste any time, do they,' said Clive, as Brendan handed him the draft contract from Mr Cheung's lawyers.

'No, and they'll expect the same quick turnaround from us, so step on it. Melissa's in the office today so you can brief her. We'll need a lot more writing from her to meet the terms of this contract. You can tell her Harveys have withdrawn their offer, so if she wants a good income in future she needs to sign this contract.'

'Right, I'll talk to her,' said Tony. 'I'll leave the contract to you and your legal people, Clive.'

Clive nodded. 'I'll need to give this a thorough check.'

'Thorough, but fast,' warned Brendan.

'Yes. I'll impress on them that time is of the essence. Melissa will want a new contract. Any change to her terms?'

'She'll want more money, but she'll only get more if she writes more. Keep her on the same percentage, but tell her there will be more sales so she'll gain overall. As we all will,' added Brendan, grinning. 'Don't let her know we're in a hurry. Just make sure she knows it's in her interests to sign her contract. We'll do the rest.'

'Got it,' said Clive, as he and Tony left Brendan's office.

Oh, what is it now, thought Brendan as his phone rang. 'Yes? McManners here. Oh, yes, it's about my garage, and some valuable books. Yes, I had specified them when I renewed my insurance at the end of last year. I'm expecting you to honour the full amount.' Brendan listened, tapping his fingers impatiently as he was taken painstakingly through a set of standard questions. *Pen-pushers*, he thought as he snapped back with his answers.

'Melissa! You're looking as glamorous as ever,' exclaimed Tony as he saw her walking up the stairs to complete the filming. 'How's the filming going? You'll be fab, I know!' he said.

'Of course I'm *fab*, Tony,' replied Melissa, flicking back her hair and flashing her trademark red nail polish.

She must have the stuff stock-piled, thought Tony. *The police would have kept the bottle that was found here.* But he kept his thoughts to himself.

'Indeed,' he continued. 'Do you have time for a quick word? I've got some rather good news.'

'That makes a change. It's been gloom and doom here for far too long. Good news for me, I assume?'

'Of course. Come into my office and I'll explain.'

Melissa looked around for somewhere to sit. Paper or books covered every surface. Tony hurriedly moved a teetering pile off one of the chairs so she could sit down.

'Now, as I said, I have good news,' he said as he moved round to sit behind his desk.

'Yes, yes,' said Melissa. 'What news?'

'As you know, we have been negotiating with a publisher in China, with a view to publishing your *Granny Fi* stories with them. And now, we've got the agreement of a very reputable and successful publisher in China. We've just received their draft contract.'

'Finally! About time. What does it mean for me?'

'The opportunity for more sales …'

'And a greater royalty,' added Melissa.

'Through increased sales,' said Tony.

'No increase in royalty? You won't get far without me,' said Melissa.

'You are our highly valued author, Melissa, but we can't increase the royalty just yet. However, Cheung is confident that *Granny Fi* will sell well in China, with the new illustrations, of course.'

'Of course. Kaye's were never going to work for them. Just as well she's out of the way.'

'Er, yes, indeed,' said Tony. 'We all miss Kaye and her work very much.'

'Hmm, I suppose so. So how many books does Cheung think he can sell?'

'He'll start with ten thousand of the existing stories, and will take whatever you can write over the next twelve months. So, the more you write, the more you will earn in royalties.'

'Not bad. I can write a book a month, so you're going to be busy.'

'Splendid. I'll get Clive and legal to draw up a contract for you.'

'Good, look forward to it. While I think of it, what happened to that takeover attempt from Harveys?'

'Harveys? They've pulled out. Which means it's all the more important to work with China.'

'I see. Well, I must get back to my filming now. A bore, but it has to be done. My public will expect it.'

'I'm sure they'll love the new videos. I'm looking forward to seeing them.'

With another flick of her hair, Melissa left the office, her heels clicking smartly away as she went out of the office and down the stairs to the room where Sam was waiting.

By 6pm, the filming was finally finished. Feeling exhausted, Sam had just enough energy to remain polite, despite Melissa's constant need for reassurance and praise. It had been a trying day, but the videos would be good. Melissa's high standards, whatever the motivation, would pay off.

Her phone pinged, and she picked up a text from Nate. He also had an appointment for a DNA test, and was checking in to see if she had one too. She updated him quickly, but she wasn't really in the mood for being sociable.

Chapter Sixteen

Tuesday, February 1st

After a good night's sleep Sam felt better, and ready to face the new day. The thought of not having to contend with Melissa made her feel less reluctant to emerge from under her duvet. She went in to the office, and left soon after for her DNA appointment.

Arriving at the police station, the duty officer asked her to wait until she was called in to give her sample. She sat quietly, checking her phone for messages. Suddenly the outer door banged open, and Jack Henshaw burst through the door. Walking past her he suddenly realised who was sitting in the waiting area, and turned to face Sam, grinning.

'We really must stop meeting like this, Sam Holliday. Or perhaps we should make a habit of it, as you clearly can't stay away from me? After all, we were in the habit of meeting, weren't we? Co-habiting in fact,' he added with a leer.

Sam looked up at him, her face a mixture of anger, disgust, and fear.

'Jack, just go away,' she said.

'Oooh, still not feeling very friendly, I see,' said Jack. 'You used to like seeing me. You used to like me,' he said, his anger increasing with every word.

'Jack, leave me alone.'

'Leave *you* alone? It's you who can't keep away from *me*,' he said, jabbing his finger at her face.

'What's going on here?' asked a uniformed woman with the rank of Inspector.

'Nothing, ma'am. Just having a few words with my girlfriend,' said Jack.

'It sounds to me as though she'd prefer not to have anything to do with you. Is that right?' the woman asked Sam.

Jack looked at Sam, daring her to say anything that might damage his reputation with this woman.

'Er, yes. Yes, it is,' said Sam, avoiding eye contact with Jack.

'Right, we'll discuss your behaviour in my office—now,' said the Inspector. Turning to Sam, she added 'If there's anything you want to tell me, just ask the duty officer to call me.'

'Thank you,' said Sam.

Jack started to follow the Inspector then turned back and hissed at Sam.

'See what you've done now? This is all *your* doing,' and he walked on quickly to catch up with the Inspector.

Same old Jack, thought Sam, remembering why she'd had to leave him. Still feeling shaky from the encounter, she reminded herself that she no longer had to put up with his bullying behaviour on a daily basis, even if she couldn't get him out of her life completely.

'Sam Holliday?' called a police officer. 'Come through, this won't take long.'

Within minutes, Sam was heading back to the office. As soon as Sam got to her desk, Jen popped her head over the desk screen and told Sam that Stacey was looking for her.

'Given away your DNA yet?' asked Jen, and Sam confirmed she had.

'I think everyone will have done it by the end of today. Wonder when we'll hear any more?' asked Jen.

Chapter Sixteen

'Maybe the end of the week? I've no idea. This is all new to me!' replied Sam. 'I'm just popping up to see Stacey. Coffee later?'

Sam stepped quietly into Stacey's office. 'Hi, how are you? It seems ages since I saw you, and so much has happened!'

'I'm fine, thanks. I just wondered if you knew anything more about Frank's letter? Inspector Keld collected the original, but is there any news? I mean, Frank thought he was going to die, and now Enid's been arrested for attempted murder. Balinski said it wasn't for Kaye's murder, so what's going on?'

'I don't really know much more, but I don't think the police believe Frank's death was suspicious.'

'What makes you say that?' asked Stacey.

'I think we would have heard something by now if Enid or someone else was going to be charged with his death. And they released Brendan, so they can't believe he was responsible for killing Frank.' She looked directly at Stacey who didn't look entirely convinced. 'We'll just have to wait and see. Even if we ask the police, I doubt they'd tell us anything. They'll just say they're 'investigating a number of lines of enquiry.'

'You've been watching too many TV detective series,' Stacey said with a small smile. 'But I suppose you're right. It's just so unsettling.'

'I know,' said Sam. 'I think all we can do is try to get on with some work.'

'As Tony told us to,' said Stacey with a rueful grin.

'Sorry, I don't mean to sound unsympathetic. My head keeps going round and round with what's been happening, but trying to focus on work does seem to help. A bit, at least.'

'There's not much else we can do, is there,' said Stacey. 'OK, let me know if there's any news.'

As Sam came out of Stacey's office, she heard Melissa's voice further along the corridor.

'OK then Clive, if your legal people have approved it, let's get it signed now. You're right, 'snail mail' will only slow things down.'

Sam heard Clive's mumbled reply. Suddenly, she knew she had to find a way to confront Melissa about the comment Anoushka had made about Melissa trying to win Kaye round. But how? She hurried to catch Melissa before she went into Clive's office.

'Hi, Melissa! So glad I've caught you. Just wondered if you'd like to have a look at the full set of videos before you go back to Manchester? Do you have time?'

'I suppose I could,' Melissa replied with a gleam in her eye that belied her hesitation. 'Yes, after I've dealt with this paperwork. You, young lady, are going to be very busy over the next few months.'

'Great!' said Sam, putting on her enthusiastic face. Perhaps the China contract had come off, she wondered. 'I'll be at my desk when you're ready.'

But Sam didn't return to her desk. Spinning through the revolving doors she left the building, and walked briskly around the corner. Taking out her phone, she called Inspector Keld and explained that she thought Melissa might have visited Kaye to try to persuade her to pursue sales in China. 'I'm going to see her in a few minutes, at my house. I'll let you know if I find out anything interesting.'

'Don't let her suspect you know anything, and do not on any account confront her. That's our job. You have no idea how she'll react, and we don't want another death on our hands.'

'Understood,' replied Sam, but Keld had already put his phone down.

Sam quickly retraced her steps, getting back to her desk before Melissa appeared. Judging by the smirk on her face, the meeting with Clive had gone well.

'Hi again,' said Sam with a bright smile. 'I'm really sorry, but there's going to be a lot of noise in here any time now—something to do with the investigation,' Sam improvised. 'Would you have time to come back to my place to look at the videos? It'll be quiet there, and the coffee's better.'

'Hmm, well it can't be any worse than the stuff they have here. Really, I hope they'll start buying something better when …' Melissa caught Sam's eye and tailed off.

'When …?' queried Sam.

'When, when someone next buys the next lot of coffee of course!' said Melissa.

'Of course. Right then, shall we make a move?'

'Oh, very well. Is it far?' asked Melissa.

'A short walk,' replied Sam, thinking it might feel longer for Melissa in her high heels.

Opening the front door of her house for Melissa to go in, Sam gritted her teeth as Melissa cooed over how sweet her 'little house' was. Sam refused to take the bait. Yes, her house was small, but it was hers (and the bank's), and she liked it.

'I'll set my laptop up on the kitchen bar while I make some coffee,' said Sam.

'Fine. Black for me. You can always tell the true quality of the coffee when it's not masked by milk or sugar.'

'Very true. I hope it will be to your taste,' said Sam, resisting the urge to spit into Melissa's cup.

'So where are these videos you're so keen to show me?, asked Melissa.

'I'll pull up the files for you. You can watch them in any order, just like someone coming to our website might view them.'

'Hmm, OK,' replied Melissa.

'They've not been edited yet, of course. You just need to double click to open each one…'

'I am computer literate, you know,' interrupted Melissa.

'Great. Coffee's coming up.'

Melissa worked her way through the videos, smiling from time to time as she watched herself say something she thought particularly good.

'Well, I think I did an excellent job. You'll be glad I insisted on doing these, now there will be more *Granny Fi* stories coming out.'

'More stories? That's great, although I am a little surprised as we no longer have Kaye for the illustrations,' Sam said.

'Huh, you're forgetting, I'm the force behind those books. They were my idea, my creation, and without me Little Bear would be nowhere.'

'Have you got some ideas for the new stories? And who will illustrate them, now that Kaye's no longer around?' asked Sam.

'Oh, I've got plenty of ideas. The stories are for the China market, which Kaye was dead against.'

Sam winced at the choice of words as Melissa carried on talking.

'I tried to persuade her that it was in her interests to sell into China. The boys were already in discussions to co-publish with a reputable Chinese children's book publisher, but she wasn't having it. Luckily, I'm not far away from that hovel she lived in, in the middle of nowhere.'

'You went there to talk to her?' asked Sam.

'She rarely answers the phone so I had no choice,' said Melissa.

'Do you know why she was so against selling into China?'

'She said we made more than enough from sales in the UK. And she knew she'd have to change the way she drew Granny Fi for the Chinese publisher, and she hated the thought of doing that. I told her to get over herself. It wouldn't be much work to change the illustrations. And the sales in the UK were dropping off. I would have thought she'd like more money to top up her pension. But she wasn't having any of it.'

'No, she was very proud of her illustrations,' said Sam.

Melissa gave Sam a sharp look. 'You knew her?'

'Not really,' Sam replied. 'I went to see her the day before she died and she showed me her illustrations. For her, Granny Fi could only look the way she had drawn her over the years.'

'You must have been one of the last people to see her,' said Melissa.

'I was staying at the pub when it happened, but yes, I probably was. When did you see her?' asked Sam.

'Before she died, obviously,' replied Melissa. 'So, are you 'helping the police with their enquiries'?'

'I was interviewed and had to make a statement, if that's what you mean,' replied Sam.

'What did the police make of it?' asked Melissa.

'They've confirmed that she died as a result of a blow to her head,' replied Sam.

'Accident or murder though?'

'I've no idea. What do you think?' replied Sam.

'Me? How should I know? Are you accusing me? You know nothing,' said Melissa, pointing her finger with its red painted nail at Sam's face, making Sam back away. As she did so, Sam tripped over the lead to her laptop.

'Careful now,' said Melissa, catching her arm. 'Don't want to end up the same way as Kaye, do you?'

Melissa's face was close to Sam's, and her hand was tight around Sam's arm. Sam made herself look into Melissa's eyes, and she saw how angry Melissa was. She tried to keep her breath even and to say as calmly as she could 'You can let go of me now. Thanks for catching me. I might have banged my head. Ah, that's the doorbell. I'd better answer it.'

Melissa gave her a hard look, and reluctantly let go of Sam's arm. 'Off you go then.'

'Oh, DC Chaudhury! Would you like to come in? Melissa Bingley's here with me: we're just looking through the videos Melissa kindly made for Little Bear to promote the *Granny Fi* series.'

DC Chaudhury looked a little taken aback at this rush of information. 'I just wanted to make sure you were OK, Sam. Your colleague reported you'd been in the office and then disappeared. She said you were going to meet up with her for a coffee, and given recent events she was a bit worried. DS Balinski thought it best to make sure you were OK.'

'I'm fine, thanks. Would you like to come in a minute? Melissa will be leaving soon, and I'll be going back to the office.'

'No, thanks, not unless you need me?' replied DC Chaudhury.

'No, no. Oh, Melissa, you're off now, are you?' said Sam, as Melissa pushed her to one side to get out of the front door.

'I've wasted enough time here. If I go now, I'll catch the next train. I really think it's about time Little Bear provided me with a driver,' said Melissa, pulling her coat around her.

'Who are you?' she asked DC Chaudhury.

'I'm Detective Constable Chaudhury, working with Detective Sargeant Balinski to investigate recent events at Little Bear.'

'Humph,' said Melissa. 'Waste of time. Everyone needs to get back to work. We've got books to sell! Out of my way!' and she pushed her way onto the pavement, walking quickly in the direction of the station.

'Ms Bingley?' called DC Chaudhury. Melissa turned round. 'You have provided your DNA, haven't you?'

'Indeed I have not, and will not until I am given a good reason to do so,' and Melissa turned back to continue walking to the station.

DC Chaudhury looked a little taken aback.

'Don't worry, she's always like that,' reassured Sam.

'And you? Are you really all right?' asked DC Chaudhury.

'Yes …,' said Sam.

'I sense a 'but'' said DC Chaudhury. 'Perhaps I should come in after all?'

'Please do,' said Sam, and she led the way to the kitchen. She was about to clear away the coffee mugs when she had a sudden thought. 'Melissa drank from this mug, so it will have her DNA, won't it?'

'Good thinking,' said DC Chaudhury. 'I'll just get a bag to put it in. Don't touch it.' She went out to her car and returned with a zip-lock plastic bag and plastic gloves. Putting on the gloves she carefully picked up the mug and placed it in the bag, sealing and labelling it. 'Now, what did you want to tell me? And please, you can call me Meera.'

'Thank you, Meera.' Sam paused. 'I don't know where to start. Nothing's happened exactly but … Melissa really is acting very oddly, even for her. I don't know her very well, but it doesn't feel right.'

'Go with your gut,' advised DC Chaudhury.

Sam looked at her gratefully. 'Well, first of all someone told me that Melissa had said she would win Kaye round, I mean, about publishing *Granny Fi* to sell into China.'

'Ah, so this is about Kaye Butterworth? I think you should speak directly to Inspector Keld about that, as he's in charge of that investigation. I'm investigating the incidents at Little Bear, involving Enid Price.'

'OK. I've got his number. He interviewed me because I was staying in the village where Kaye lived the night she died. I'll call him now.'

Inspector Keld answered after the first ring. 'Keld.'

'Inspector Keld, it's Sam Holliday here.'

'Are you all right?'

'I am, but there are a few things I need to tell you. I'm at home, and DC Chaudhury is here. She's working with DS Balinski on the Little Bear investigation.'

'Continue,' said Keld.

'This might sound a bit jumbled, but I think it might be important.'

'I'm listening,' said Keld.

'Well, you know I met the woman who used to do my job at Little Bear. And you know about the plans to co-publish the *Granny Fi* stories with a publisher in China?'

'Yes, to both. Publishing in China is not a crime, however,' replied Keld.

'No, of course not. But this woman—she's called Anoushka—told me that Melissa, the author of the *Granny Fi* books was really keen to publish for China, and that Kaye was not. According to Anoushka, Melissa was very angry with Kaye, and said she'd win her round. That's why I phoned you last time, because I was going to see if I could find out from Melissa what she meant.'

'Yes, and I told you to be careful.'

'I was … well, maybe not that careful.' Sam sighed. 'I suggested she came to my house to look at the videos we'd been making to promote her books.'

'Hmm,' said Keld. 'Go on,' he said, as Sam paused.

'I thought it would give us a chance to talk, and perhaps I could get her talking about Kaye. She told me about publishing for China. She was really enthusiastic about that, and told me it was going ahead. She also said that Kaye had been against selling into China, as we know. She said she went to see Kaye to try to talk her round, but, as Melissa put it, Kaye 'wasn't having it.'

'I asked her when she'd seen Kaye and that was when she—Melissa that is—got a bit rattled with me, and started jabbing her finger into my face. I stepped back and tripped over a lead. Melissa grabbed my arm and said 'you wouldn't want to go the same way as Kaye, would you.' She looked so angry. And then the doorbell rang so she had to let me go. She really spooked me though. Oh, and she hasn't given her DNA but she had a coffee at my place, so DC Chaudhury's got the mug to use for testing.'

'An eventful morning,' commented Keld. 'You took a risk, and luckily you're safe. What you've told me is very helpful indeed. I'll need to ask Ms Bingley some further questions. Where is she now?'

'Heading for the train station to go back to Manchester,' replied Sam.

'We'll meet her at the Manchester end,' said Keld.

'Right. Do you think she killed Kaye?'

'I can't answer that, but I need to talk to her about her visit to Miss Butterworth's house. Did she tell you when that was?'

'No .... No, she didn't. She said something about it. Oh, yes, she was a bit sarcastic and said it was before Kaye died. Not a lot of help. But that was when she suddenly got so angry.'

'Interesting. I'll look into it. You've been most helpful, Miss Holliday. And now, please leave any further questions to me. You put yourself in danger today.'

'I know, and you did warn me. I'm going back to the office in a minute, and I'll spend the rest of the day there,' replied Sam.

'Good,' and Keld ended the call.

'Someone's going to meet the Manchester train. The Inspector wants to talk to Melissa,' Sam explained to Meera. 'I expect he'll be in touch with DS Balinski, to update him.'

'That's good. Right, do you really want to go back to the office?' asked Meera.

'I do. I'd rather be busy,' said Sam.

'I'll walk with you,' said Meera.

'Oh, there's no need,' replied Sam.

'I'd just like to make sure Melissa isn't waiting round the corner.'

'Oh! I hadn't thought of that! Do you think she might be?'

'She's quite unpredictable,' said Meera. 'I'm going into town so it's on my way.'

Sam wasn't entirely convinced, but she suddenly felt glad to have Meera with her. 'I'd better have that coffee with Jen and stop her worrying about me,' said Sam.

Nate stood up, stretched, and looked out of the window. It was almost dark, and although his house was not overlooked, it would feel cosier with the curtains drawn. As he moved towards the window, a car drove past and stopped. People arriving to stay in one of the rental properties, perhaps? Surely no one for Kaye. Curiosity piqued, he picked up Gustav's lead and called the dog to him. 'How about a walk, Gustav?' Gustav's tail waved dutifully, and he walked slowly to the door. 'Your heart's still not in it, is it, old chap,' said Nate as he patted the dog's head. 'Come on, let's make sure all's well with the new arrivals.' Gustav woofed his agreement, and headed out of the open door into the quiet evening.

A silver-grey car was parked further along the road, but whoever had been in it had disappeared. Gustav automatically turned left for his usual walk, but Nate gently tugged the lead to direct him the opposite way. Gustav hesitated, looking up at Nate to make sure he really did mean to go a different way, and reluctantly went to the right towards his old home. *At least he's not trying to run back to Kaye's* thought Nate.

As they walked along the road, Nate noticed the holiday homes were in darkness, but there was a flickering light in Kaye's house. Who was in there, and why? There was only one way to find out.

Nate walked towards the house, treading quietly as he got closer. He could see nothing in the front window, so he went cautiously to the back door. It was boarded it up, to cover the smashed window pane where Nate had broken into the house a few nights ago.

He could see through the back-room window. Hanging back in the shadows, Nate looked in. He could see a figure kneeling at Kaye's desk, running their hands underneath the drawers. Gustav growled, and placing a hand on his head to quieten him, Nate felt the fur on the back of Gustav's head rise and his body tense. Who could it be? Suddenly, the figure moved, and Nate instinctively stepped further back and waited. Nothing. He moved carefully, looking through the window once again. The person had gone, and the light was now in an upstairs room. It couldn't be the police. They would turn the lights on. A burglar, perhaps? Had someone been watching the house and figured no one was living there?

Gustav's body was rigid with tension. Nate gently smoothed the dog's head to calm him, and himself. Should he challenge the intruder, or simply call the police? He decided to make the call, looking up to the windows above to see if he could work out what was happening.

'Emergency services. Which service do you require?'

'Police,' said Nate, quietly.

'Can you give me an address, and a reason for the call?'

'Yes, but I need to speak very quietly,' replied Nate.

'Are you in danger?'

'Not at the moment, but there's someone in my neighbour's house, moving around inside with what looks like a torch. My neighbour was killed a few days ago.'

'Where are you?'

Nate gave the address, and was assured a police car would be there shortly.

'I advise you to return to your house. On no account enter the building, or challenge this person. The police will take it from here.'

'Understood,' said Nate. He moved quietly back to the road,

and tried to walk normally, talking quietly to Gustav who was pulling on the lead to return to his old home.

'No, Gustav, it's not your home now. Come on, let's get back in the warm.' He felt relieved when Gustav picked up his pace and they were soon back indoors.

Nate sat on the sofa, listening for an approaching car. Time stood still. As Gustav's ears pricked, Nate picked up the sound of car tyres on the road. No siren, no flashing lights. He looked out of his window and saw the distinctive livery of a police car. Two people got out, and moved towards Kaye's house. Nate's phone pinged. He glanced at the screen and saw it was text message from Sam. He glanced back at the road. Nothing happening, so he opened the message and read Sam's message.

Melissa told me she went to Kaye's house to try to persuade her to publish Granny Fi in China, but Kaye wouldn't change her mind. M got really angry with me—scary! Keld is going to talk to her. All quiet with you?

Nate smiled. It was quiet, but it probably wouldn't be for much longer. He decided to step outside with Gustav again. Gustav sighed as though two outings in an evening was really asking too much. Nate gave a quick glance along the road. No one. As he walked towards Kaye's house, the policemen came out with a woman. Walking either side of her, the police were holding on to the woman's arms. Gustav stopped, growling.

'Melissa!' exclaimed Nate. 'Is everything all right?'

'Does it look it? Who the hell are you?' replied Melissa.

'Kaye's neighbour, Nate Braithwaite.'

'Never heard of you. Get that dreadful hound out of my way,' said Melissa as Gustav growled even louder, baring his teeth.

One of the policemen raised his eyebrows at Nate, making his opinion of Melissa very plain. 'Sorry sir, but we need to get this woman into the car. I suggest you return home.'

'I'll do that. Is everything all right at the house? As I said, I'm a neighbour. Gustav, sssh,' Nate said to the now barking Gustav.

'A nosy neighbour. And that's Kaye's ghastly dog!' said Melissa, kicking out at Gustav and trying to free her arms from the policemen's hold. As she did so, several pieces of paper fell out of the sleeve of her coat. Nate bent to pick them up.

'That's Kaye's writing,' he said. 'You were hiding these. You must have taken them from Kaye's house!'

'Oh, you really are a nosy neighbour, aren't you. Or are you police as well? Well, no comment,' said Melissa.

Nate glanced down again at the top piece of paper. It was a story. 'These are *Granny Fi* stories,' said Nate in surprise.

'Aren't you smart?' said Melissa. 'Yes, they are *Granny Fi* stories. Which means they belong to me. I haven't *stolen* anything.'

'But why were they at Kaye's house?' asked Nate.

'Because they are MINE,' insisted Melissa.

'We'll take it from here, sir. Wait here while we get her in the car,' said one of the policemen. Nate waited as Melissa was manoeuvred into the waiting car, and one of the policeman slid into the driver's seat. The other turned back to speak to Nate. Gustav stopped barking and stood quietly.

'Right then, sir, I'll need to take those papers. You shouldn't have looked at them, you know,' the policemen said.

'I'm sorry, it was just instinctive. You know she's a children's storybook author? Melissa Bingley? She wrote the stories, and my neighbour, Kaye Butterworth, drew the illustrations. I met Melissa once or twice when she came to Kaye's house, although she doesn't seem to remember me. A few days ago, Kaye died here, in her house—in suspicious circumstances.'

'Thank you, sir, that's very useful. And your name again?'

'Nate Braithwaite. I live at the cottage with the lights on. I made the call to the emergency services this evening.'

'I see. Best go home now, sir. Someone will come to talk to you tomorrow.'

'Inspector Keld is in charge of the Kaye Butterworth case. He knows me, and has my phone number.'

'Good—and goodnight, sir,' said the policeman, walking round to get into the passenger seat of the car.

'Come on then, Gustav. Home again, and this time we'll stay there!' Gustav looked up at him and almost smiled.

Chapter Sixteen

Putting the kettle on to make some tea, Nate remembered the text from Sam. Presumably Sam was OK but he'd better check.

Hope you're OK? Melissa was in Kaye's cottage just now. She's been arrested!

Within a couple of minutes his phone pinged with Sam's reply.

Keld was going to pick her up from Manchester station. She said she was getting the train back. She must have had the car and planned to drive to Kaye's —why was she lying?

No idea, but she had a bunch of Granny Fi stories literally up her sleeves replied Nate.

What? Sam replied.

Yep. Talk soon? asked Nate.

Yes. Let's talk tomorrow. There might be more news by then! replied Sam.

Chapter Seventeen

Wednesday, February 2nd

Sam woke with a start, feeling disorientated and with her heart hammering. It was a dream, a bad dream. She tried to catch the memory of it. Melissa. Yes, Melissa was clutching a pile of *Granny Fi* stories, and Sam was shouting at her. But why? Because .... Because the stories were not Melissa's. Then whose were they?

Sam couldn't remember. Perhaps a cup of tea would help. It was still early, so she brought her tea back to bed and snuggled under the duvet, thinking. *What if … what if it wasn't Melissa who wrote the stories? What if Kaye had written them? But why? Was she reading too much into her dream?*

It was time to get herself moving if she was going to get to the office on time. She decided she would call Inspector Keld just before she left for work. She had a feeling he kept early hours.

With her work things to hand, Sam rang Keld's number. As she expected, after a couple of rings she heard the now familiar 'Keld'.

'Good morning, Inspector. It's Sam Holliday here.'

'And Melissa Bingley is now here, with us, in custody,' replied Keld with a note of satisfaction. 'She wasn't on the train. She drove from Lower Rushford, but not to Manchester. We picked her up in Upper Braithwaite, thanks to Nate.'

'I heard from Nate. He saw she was arrested at Kaye's house yesterday evening.'

'She was. I'll be questioning her shortly. Hopefully by then I'll have the DNA results.'

'I've … well, I've been thinking that some things just don't feel right.'

'Go on,' said Keld.

'What if Melissa wasn't the author of the *Granny Fi* stories? It looks as though she went back to Kaye's house last night specifically to get those stories. But why were they in Kaye's cottage? Why didn't Melissa have them already, and why did she have to break in to steal them?'

'Good questions. I'll be asking her about all that, and plenty more. I've another call coming in. I'll get back to you when I have any news.'

Keld ended the call and answered the new, incoming one.

'Good morning, Nate. I hear you were a little out of order last night. But thanks for raising the alarm. Saved us having to track her down,' said Keld.

'Yes, sorry about that, but it's a good thing you've brought her in. I think she's a bit unhinged. And she really puts Gustav's back up —well, his fur anyway. I've never seen him react to anyone like that before.'

'Interesting,' said Keld. 'Is there anything else you wanted to tell me?'

'No, just that I thought Gustav's reaction was something you should know about.'

'I'm very grateful to you and to Gustav. I'm hoping that by the end of today this case will be closed.'

'Good,' said Nate, but Keld had already gone.

Chapter Seventeen

Keld opened his office door and called out to his team in the open-plan office. 'Any news on the DNA test, any of you? Bingley's, or the Lower Rushford people?'

'Yes, sir,' answered one of Keld's team. 'It's all on the system.'

'Right,' said Keld, entering his password on his computer. He found the batch of results related to the Kaye Butterworth case and cast his eye down the list, stopping at Melissa Bingley. 'Interesting,' he said to himself. 'Very interesting.'

Keld looked through the papers that Melissa Bingley wanted so badly that she'd broken in to her dead colleague's house and stolen them. Sam Holliday had queried whether Melissa was the author of these stories. But why did that matter? They were just stories: stories that had made the publisher, the author, and presumably the illustrator a great deal of money.

And then he found it. Tucked between the last two stories was a note.

> *Melissa*
>
> *These are the last stories I'll write. I do not owe you anything more. I will not write stories for Granny Fi to be published in China. I'll take a chance you won't carry out your threats. After all, you've as much to lose as I have after all these years.*
>
> *Kaye*

So Kaye Butterworth was both author and illustrator. Why did that have to be a secret? Another question for Melissa.

She really was the most exasperating woman, but Keld had interviewed more difficult people than Melissa. When she wasn't extolling her own virtues as a talented author, she was refusing to say anything other than 'no comment'. *It would be easy to annoy her*, thought Keld, *perhaps to the extent that she would say more than she intended.*

'You claim to be a famous author,' said Keld.

'It's not a claim. I *am* a famous author,' replied Melissa.

'Are you?' asked Keld.

'Of course I am. The success of the *Granny Fi* series speaks for itself. How dare you challenge it,' said Melissa.

'I'm simply trying to get to the truth,' said Keld. 'Because you're not the author of that series, are you?'

'What?' said Melissa. 'How dare you!' She stabbed her finger at Keld. 'Who the hell do you think wrote those stories?'

'I think Kaye Butterworth wrote them,' said Keld.

'Rubbish! All she could do was draw!' replied Melissa.

'No, she could write. In fact, she wrote you a letter, didn't she,' said Keld.

'A letter?'

'Yes. This letter,' said Keld, giving the details for the recording. 'Read it out, please, for the recording, and to jog your memory.'

Her solicitor whispered to Melissa but Melissa elbowed her away. Leaning over the interview table Melissa pointed her red-tipped finger at Keld.

'That bitch. After all I did for her,' said Melissa.

'Tell me,' said Keld.

'No comment,' prompted Melissa's solicitor. Melissa flapped a hand at her.

'No, I'll tell you. I wrote those stories, years ago, but the Little Bear editors thought they needed further work. I don't do 'further work'. My stories are perfect as they are. But Kaye meddled with them as she drew the illustrations, and Little Bear loved what she did. So, I'd give her some ideas for the stories, then Kaye drew the pictures and wrote the text. Everyone was happy.'

'What changed?' asked Keld.

'Kaye had an affair with Charlotte's husband,' said Melissa.

'Who is Charlotte?' asked Keld.

'Kaye's sister, Charlotte McManners. She started the Little Bear company with Kaye, and their first successful series was my *Granny Fi.*'

'Carry on,' said Keld.

The solicitor placed a restraining hand on Melissa.

'Get off me, I'm going to tell my side of the story,' said Melissa.

'I have warned you not to say anything,' said her solicitor.

Melissa ignored her. 'I saw them together—Kaye and Charlotte's husband—so when Kaye got pregnant, I knew who the father was. It would have meant the end of Charlotte's marriage, and probably of Little Bear if word got out. I said I'd keep quiet. Andrew—Charlotte's husband, didn't want anything to do with the baby. He wanted to do whatever was least likely to jeopardise his marriage . He had a lot to lose if he and Charlotte separated. He told Kaye to get rid of the baby, but Kaye didn't want to do that. She had a cottage in Cumbria, so I told her to set herself up there and keep a low profile. She'd tell her sister about the pregnancy but not that her brother-in-law was the father.

Charlotte and Andrew didn't have any children at that time. Charlotte was desperate for a baby and somehow, she got Andrew to agree to adopt Kaye's child, not knowing it was also Andrew's own child. That child is Brendan McManners. When Charlotte and Andrew's own baby, Frank, was born a few years later, they brought the boys up as brothers.'

'And what did Kaye have to do in return?' asked Keld.

'Write the stories. She liked meddling with them, so she may as well write them all. The ideas were all mine. She just wrote the words. Writing's a bore, especially when you're asked to do 'further work',' said Melissa.

'What was going to happen if Little Bear decided to co-publish with the company in China?'

'Kaye would need to write more stories. But she refused,' said Melissa.

'What did you do?' asked Keld.

'I went to see her. Tried to talk her round, but she didn't want to know. She said we had enough sales in the UK, and that she didn't want to start changing Granny Fi for a new market.'

'So, your supply of stories was about to dry up, just as you had the opportunity to make more money from a series you contributed nothing towards,' said Keld.

'Granny Fi was *my* creation. Kaye just made up the stories based on my ideas and drew the pictures. Without me, there would be nothing,' said Melissa.

'How did you feel when Kaye refused to change her mind about China?'

'Annoyed.'

'Was that all? Weren't you furious?' asked Keld.

'Humph. I suppose I was,' said Melissa.

'The letter mentions threats,' said Keld.

'I said I'd reveal she had an illegitimate child, and I'd name the child, and his father,' said Melissa, looking pleased with herself.

'How did you kill her?' asked Keld.

'I didn't. I just gave her a little push and she tripped over that blasted dog, fell backwards, and banged her head on the hearth-stone. God, the blood. And that hound! I thought it was going to attack me. I had to get out.'

'Without checking whether you could do anything for Kaye?'

'It looked terminal to me. And if I'd stayed, the dog would have killed me too,' shuddered Melissa.

Trying to mask his disgust, Keld said 'You're not telling the whole truth, are you? Your DNA matches the DNA we took from the hair that was in Kaye's hands when she died.'

'What DNA?' asked Melissa, looking at Keld in disbelief. 'I didn't give my sample for testing.'

'And now we know why. However, we found it by other means,' said Keld.

'That damned marketing woman! You got it from the mug of coffee I had at her house. The conniving, deceitful ....'

'I'd stop there, if I were you,' advised Keld. 'Yes, we have your DNA. That was no little push. There must have been a tussle, because strands of your hair were found under Kaye's nails. You meant her to go down, and to stay there.'

'No comment,' said Melissa.

'Did you take Miss Butterworth's drawings the night you killed her, or did you go back later?'

Melissa looked at him in disbelief. 'I told you; the dog was about to tear me to shreds. I wasn't hanging around for that to happen. No, I went back one night when you lot weren't around. I had to wait a few days for everything to quieten down.'

'Why did you want the drawings?' asked Keld.

'I didn't. I wanted to see if she'd written any more stories, or if she'd written anything to me.'

'And did you find anything?' asked Keld.

'Not until I went back there yesterday. You know I found her letter. Not only was she blocking sales to China, but she was reneging on our agreement!' Melissa's face was flushed with anger.

Keld looked at her, and reached a decision. 'Melissa Bingley, I'm charging you with the murder of Kaye Butterworth so listen carefully to what I'm about to say.'

'You!' said Melissa, turning to her solicitor. 'You're supposed to ensure this didn't happen. You're useless!'

'I did warn you, several times, but you insisted on telling your story,' shrugged the solicitor. 'Inspector Keld is within his rights to charge you. I'm afraid I won't be able to represent you from here. You'll have to find someone else.'

'You can't just walk out on me!' said Melissa.

'Watch me,' said the solicitor, as the door was unlocked for her to leave.

'Melissa Bingley,' said Keld, 'I'm arresting you ….'

For once, Melissa had nothing to say.

Sam kept checking her phone to see if she'd missed a message from Inspector Keld but there was nothing from him, just a message from her mother saying it had been a while since she'd heard from Sam, and another from Nate asking if she had any news. The working day passed slowly without any further messages, and Sam eventually packed away her things to go home.

Chopping up a butternut squash to make soup proved a good way to deal with a frustrating and difficult day. Once she'd added the spices and set it to cook, she tried to settle on the sofa with a cup of tea, but she was too restless, checking her phone more often than was sensible. When it did finally ring, it made her jump.

'Inspector, what news?' asked Sam.

'I've charged Melissa Bingley with the murder of Kaye Butterworth,' Keld replied.

'Wow! I mean, I sort of expected it, but hearing you say it—well, I'm shocked. How could she have done that to Kaye?' said Sam.

'It's a long story. I'm coming down to Lower Rushford and I'll brief you and your colleagues tomorrow. I'm trusting you to keep this call to yourself. You played an important part in this arrest, so I thought you should know. I'm also going to notify Nate Braithwaite,' said Keld.

'Thank you, Inspector. It's a relief to know Kaye's killer has been caught. Kaye really didn't deserve to die.'

'Few murder victims do,' said Keld, and rang off.

Nate ended the call. The news of Melissa's arrest shocked him, and he immediately wanted to talk to Sam, if only to reassure himself that she was all right. It was a relief to hear her quiet voice saying 'Hi, Nate. You OK?'

'Well, yes, I suppose I am. Bit knocked sideways with Keld's news. How about you?'

Having shared all they knew about Melissa, her arrest, and going over her curious behaviour once again, Nate took a deep breath and said 'I'm thinking I might head south at the weekend.'

'Anywhere near Lower Rushford?' asked Sam, suddenly aware of how much she would like to see him.

'If you'd like me to be,' said Nate.

There was a pause. 'Yes, yes, I would like that. I mean, I'd really like to see you,' said Sam.

'Good,' said Nate. Taking a deep breath he asked 'How about dinner on Friday evening?'

'Lovely. Sounds a plan,' said Sam, smiling to herself as she ended the call, settling back into the sofa and feeling much more relaxed than when she had first come home.

Chapter Eighteen

Thursday, February 3rd

As Sam came through the revolving doors of the Little Bear offices, she was greeted by Debbie who told her that there would be a briefing with the police at 10. Sam nodded, and said she'd be there.

'I hope there's some news,' said Debbie.

'Yes, and let's hope it's good news,' said Sam as she headed for the stairs. 'See you later.'

Jen was already at her desk. Sam nodded as Jen waved a mug at her, suggesting they make coffee.

'What do you think's going to happen at the briefing?' asked Jen.

'An update?' said Sam.

'Didn't think of that one,' said Jen, giving Sam a hard look. 'Oh, I get it, you know something you can't share. OK, no more questions, m'lud. Here you go—the finest coffee you'll find at Little Bear.'

'I think when things settle down a bit, we should have another lunch at Gino's,' said Sam.

'Let's hope there'll be something to celebrate,' said Jen.

Eventually, it was time to head to the Board Room for the

briefing. Inspector Keld nodded to Sam as she came in. He was joined by DS Balinski and DC Chaudhury, and around the table was everyone who worked at Little Bear, except Clive, Tony, Brendan, and Enid.

'I'm assuming everyone who should be here, is here?' asked Inspector Keld.

'We're missing the three Board members,' said Jason Lee.

'We can go ahead without them,' said Keld. There was a ripple of surprise around the table.

'I asked you to attend the briefing this morning so we can update you on the death of Kaye Butterworth. Yesterday, Melissa Bingley was arrested and charged with her murder,' said Keld. There was a sharp intake of breath from everyone around the table before a babble of questions started.

'But why?' asked one person.

'Yes, why?' asked another. 'I don't get it. Without Kaye there won't be any more *Granny Fi* stories. Did she want to kill off the publishing as well as her illustrator?'

'Yes, what's the motive?' asked another.

Inspector Keld raised his hand for silence. 'I'm not able to tell you anything more than this: Melissa Bingley has admitted to carrying out actions that caused Kaye Butterworth's death. She has been arrested for Miss Butterworth's murder. The case will, in time, go to court, where I have every confidence that a jury will find her guilty.'

The room was silent for a moment, before more questions were asked about what would happen next, and when Melissa's case would go to trial.

'What about Kaye?' asked Jason. 'I mean, will her family be able to plan her funeral now?'

'Not yet. The coroner may need to be involved, and that could delay things considerably. We will, of course, keep her family informed,' said Keld.

Chapter Nineteen

Friday, February 4th

Sam was once again rummaging through her wardrobe. Nate had booked a restaurant in the town, and she wasn't sure what to wear. Dresses always felt too fussy. Trousers didn't seem quite right. In the end, she decided on a skirt that went well with a silky overblouse. Putting on some jewellery, she felt she'd made an effort for the evening without looking as though she was—to use an expression she hated—'on the pull'. It was going to be a cold evening, but with a warm coat and long boots she would be fine. The restaurant was walking distance so she could walk briskly to warm up.

Opening the door of the restaurant, Sam felt relieved to see that Nate was already at the table. She always hated being the first to arrive. She indicated to a hovering waiter that she was going to join him.

'Nate, it's lovely to see you,' said Sam, as she gave him a hug. 'So much has happened!'

'Good to see you too,' said Nate hugging her back. 'Now, what can I get you to drink?'

Drinks ordered, Sam commented 'I still can't take it in that it was Melissa who killed Kaye.'

'She was behaving really oddly when I saw her at Kaye's house. And Gustav hated her. I've never heard him growl and bark at anyone like that before. He knew she was responsible for killing Kaye, even if it took the rest of us a while to work it out. What did Keld say at the briefing?'

'He didn't give much away … oh, the waiter's just coming with our drinks.'

'Here's to better times,' said Nate, and they quietly tapped each other's glass. 'I wonder if we'll ever know the full story?'

'Probably not until it comes to court. And I've no idea if Little Bear will be able to carry on, or if I've got a job. Or if I'll want the job. Charlotte McManners—Brendan's mother—is talking to everyone next week. I don't know what's happened to the rest of the board. No one's seen them, and they weren't at the briefing.'

'I don't know what to wish for you, Sam—a job, or the chance to put Little Bear behind you. Whatever happens, I'm here if you need me,' said Nate, his concern for her written all over his face.

Tears suddenly welled up in Sam's eyes as she smiled her thanks, taking a sip of her wine to mask her sudden emotion.

There was a pause before Sam continued. 'I'm not sure either. I think I'll wait and see what I make of Charlotte McManners. If she's anything like Brendan, I won't hang around for long.'

'Changing the subject, I was looking at the weather for tomorrow, and it's looking good, for February. There's a book of local walks at the place where I'm staying. There's one that goes up Cleeve Hill. How about doing that tomorrow?'

'That sounds wonderful. And hopefully, this time, I won't need rescuing!' said Sam.

Nate grinned and said 'I'll have the walking poles with me, just in case!'

Chapter Twenty

Saturday, February 5th

Standing at the top of Cleeve Hill, Nate and Sam stood looking at the view spread beneath them. Breathing heavily after a brisk climb up the hill, they stood together, quietly appreciating the feeling of calm.

'OK?' asked Nate, turning to Sam and smiling. 'Got your breath back?'

'Just about!'

'Come on then, let's walk over the top and then head down to a pub,' said Nate. Instinctively, he held out his hand for Sam to take. Hand-in-hand, they made their way across the rough, stony path, both very aware of what had just happened and keeping their eyes fixed on the view. Sam's foot slid on some loose stones and she gasped.

'No, don't worry, I'm fine,' she said. They grinned at each other.

'Good,' said Nate, and squeezed her hand. 'Because I forgot the poles. Now let's go.'

Chapter Twenty-One

Monday, February 7th

Weak sunshine filtered round the edges of Sam's bedroom curtains. She stretched, luxuriating in the warmth of her bed, and feeling happy. Despite everything that had happened recently, the weekend had been a good one, and all the better for having Nate around. But now it was Monday, and she had to get to work. What would today bring?

The blinds of the Board Room were angled to let in the winter sunshine, brightening the room. Around the table were the remaining employees of Little Bear, and an older woman that few of them knew.

'Good morning, everyone. My name is Charlotte McManners. I'm ashamed to say that I have not met many of you before now. But that is going to change. As you probably know, I founded Little Bear many years ago with my sister, Kaye, who sadly is no longer with us.'

The expressions on the faces of Little Bear's staff ranged from suspicious to optimistic, from sad to curious.

Charlotte continued. 'Brendan McManners, Clive Ferguson,

and Tony Pearson have resigned, and are no longer working for Little Bear. I am creating a new limited company, to be called Phoenix Publishing. Little Bear will remain an imprint of Phoenix so we will keep the brand, but it will be a subsidiary of Phoenix. I will be the Chief Executive of the new company, and I'll be working to appoint a new Board. Any questions so far?'

'Are our jobs secure?' asked Stacey.

'If we can work together to make a success of Phoenix, then there's every chance you will all continue to have jobs. The name I've chosen—Phoenix—represents a new start, and a new approach. I want to attract new authors, and to broaden our publishing to ensure we are known for offering books that today's children beg their parents to buy. I'd welcome your ideas for writers, or types of books. I want to work much more closely with you all to ensure Phoenix is up and running quickly, and running well.' Charlotte smiled as everyone applauded.

'What about graphic novels?' asked Jen.

'e-Books?' asked Jason.

'Modern marketing?' asked Sam.

Charlotte smiled. 'I knew I could count on you all. I can't wait to get started.'

Sam caught Jen's eye. 'Lunch at Gino's?' Sam asked.

'Jumping jellybeans,' said Jen. 'Try and stop me!'

With thanks

Firstly, I am hugely grateful to Beth Kempton, of Do What You Love. I listened to one of Beth's podcasts where she talked about a book being written one scene at a time (not Beth's words!). This was a breakthrough moment for me. I was struggling to imagine how I could write anything longer than a short story, when Beth's comment showed me that a longer book can be thought of in much smaller bites. So instead of the scary prospect of having to write tens of thousands of words, I realised I could take it one small scene at a time. And so I wrote the first scene, then the next, and the next … and eventually the first Sam Holliday book appeared. Thank you, Beth!

Many, many thanks to my friends who encouraged me in my writing, reading drafts and saving me from numerous howlers. I appreciate your honesty and enthusiasm for Sam. In particular, I'd like to thank Linda Gray, Sue Rudge, Caroline Phillips, Mark McArthur-Christie, Pippa Shay, Christina Turner, and Stephanie Richards: you all gave generously of your time and helped to shape this book. Thank you.

My thanks to Richard Rudge, who enthusiastically shared his knowledge of fighting fires. I learned a lot, and any mistakes in the book are mine.

Lastly but definitely not least: Jon Franklin, thank you for all your support and encouragement, and of course for the wonderful (and usually much-needed) coffee.

Printed in Dunstable, United Kingdom

71666804R00121